INSTILLING OBEDIENCE

by

RAY GORDON

I0517538

Published by **CHIMERA**
ISBN 9781780806334

Chapter 1

Emily sat opposite her parents in the lounge, her brown eyes widening as she listened to her father in stunned silence. He was explaining the rules and regulations to Arthur, their next-door neighbour. This was extremely embarrassing for Emily. At eighteen years old she didn't need anyone to keep an eye on her while her parents were away on holiday. She didn't need babysitting. Wringing her hands as her father laid down the law, she felt her stomach sinking. She'd been looking forward to a taste of freedom, but it seemed she was going to be far from free for the next two weeks.

'Don't worry,' Arthur said, brushing back his crop of greying hair, 'I'll watch over Emily and the house.'

'No parties while we're away,' Emily's mother warned. 'And no one's to sleep over.'

'I take it I am allowed out of the house,' Emily sighed, despondently tapping her toe on the carpet.

'Of course you're allowed out, dear,' her mother replied. 'But I want you home by ten o'clock. That's quite late enough for a girl of your age with the amount of studying you've got to do.'

'Remember this, Emily,' her father said firmly, then looked out of the window at the sound of the taxi horn, 'behave yourself while we're away and you'll be allowed to go on holiday with Christine later in the summer. Look upon this as a test.'

Watching Arthur help her parents lug the suitcases out to the waiting taxi, Emily felt as though she were being treated like a child. But that wasn't unusual. Although she was an adult, a young woman, she was still a child in their eyes. They'd been in their thirties when she was born and she'd often wondered whether they'd planned to have a baby. Was she the result of a mistake? But a mistake or not she was their only child, their precious daughter, and they had trouble allowing her to grow up.

Emily's parents were old-fashioned in the extreme, and incredibly strict. So much so that she found it amazing that they should leave her alone in the house for two weeks at all. But, as her father had said, this was a test. She was really looking forward to going to Tenerife in early September with her best friend, Christine, so she was determined to pass this unfair trial.

Standing on the doorstep and waving goodbye as the taxi drove off, Emily felt a mixture of relief and anxiety. She'd hoped to have a great time while her parents were away, but with Arthur watching over her she wasn't so sure. She offered him a tight smile as he walked up the path towards her. He'd been a friend of the family for as long as she could remember. Working from home as a computer consultant, he lived alone and regularly called round for a coffee and a chat with her father.

Emily had often thought it odd that he'd never married. Despite being in his fifties he was reasonably good-looking and pretty good company. Perhaps he'd never met the right woman. And there again, he was a bit of a loner. He rarely went out or had visitors, and didn't look the type who'd enjoy a drink in the pub with the lads.

'I wish I was off to Spain,' he said, standing before Emily. 'Still, I have a lot of work to do.'

'The flight should only take a couple of hours,' she said, checking her watch.

'The flight's the easy part,' Arthur grumbled. 'It always amazes me to think that more time is spent messing around in the airport than on the aeroplane.' He focused on the fullness of her succulent lips and smiled. 'This is the first year you've not gone with them, isn't it? How do you feel?'

'I enjoyed all our holidays, but now I'm too old to build sandcastles on the beach and stuff like that.'

'So, you have two weeks to yourself. What have you got planned now?'

'Er... nothing, really,' Emily she, averting her eyes guiltily. 'I might ring Christine and see whether she wants to go out for a walk.'

'Remember you have to be home by ten.'

'Yes, yes of course.' Surely Arthur was joking?

'You know what your father's like. He'll ask me what time you went out, what time you got back. As he said, this is a bit of a test to see how you behave. Right, I'd better go and make myself something to eat and then get on with some work.'

Waiting until Arthur had returned to his house, Emily stepped back into the hall and closed the front door. She'd been waiting for this moment for several months, but now? Home by ten? Arthur wasn't serious, was he? He'd been a teenager once, she reflected; surely he wasn't going to report her every move to her parents. There again, she might have guessed that her parents weren't going to allow her even a little freedom. But at least she'd not been dragged on holiday to Spain as usual. At least that was something to be thankful for.

In her room she pulled a carrier bag out from beneath her bed and tipped its contents onto the quilt - a black leather miniskirt, a blue and white blouse, several pairs of white knickers and bras, make-up, and a scanty bikini. Running her fingertips over the cotton knickers she'd bought, she smiled. Skimpy knickers were going to make a pleasant change from the dowdy things she was used to. Holding the scanty garment to her face she felt her stomach somersault. Soft, sensual... she'd bought the clothes several days previously and had been eager to try them on, and at last the time had come.

Her mother had always bought her clothes, never allowing her to grow up. Emily had once suggested that she at least buy her own underwear, but her parents dismissed the idea scornfully. Her mother had been buying her clothes since she was a child, and nothing had changed or was going to change. Her father didn't like change. Strait-laced, staid in his ways, he didn't believe change necessary or a good thing. But at long last Emily was going to change. If only for two weeks, she was going to dress like a young woman.

Slipping out of her blue jeans and T-shirt, she slipped into her new outfit and stood before the full-length mirror. The transformation amazed her. Running her fingers through her shoulder-length auburn hair, she grinned as she eyed the reflection of an attractive young lady in the mirror. With the violin curves of her teenage body accentuated by her tight skirt and blouse, she felt really feminine for the first time in her life.

Emily was discovering herself, her individuality, her identity. She was a person in her own right, she thought happily as she focused on her shapely legs. Was the skirt too short? Other girls of her age wore short skirts. She eyed the deep cleavage of her firm breasts, the outline of her ripe nipples naughtily defined by the material of her blouse. Was it too revealing? No, her new clothes were fine. New clothes, new image. But only for two weeks. When her parents returned she'd have to hide them and resort to wearing her jeans and baggy tops again.

Checking her watch, she sat at her dressing table and applied her make-up. Just gone six o'clock. She'd be meeting Christine in the wine bar in less than an hour. If her father knew she was planning to go to a bar he'd go absolutely mad. He was against pubs and alcohol. Pop music, dancing, short skirts, make-up... it was his upbringing, Emily reflected. His father had been a vicar, a religious fanatic. Emily's mother had gone along with her husband's moralistic ideals because she'd had no choice. Had she *ever* been a teenager?

This was like being released from prison, Emily mused, glossing her pouting lips. Eye shadow, lipstick, a short skirt; all things her father had forbidden; the evils he despised. With a sense of freedom and devilish excitement coursing through her, Emily was sure her neighbour wouldn't be watching out for her when she got home. Arthur was all right, a nice man. He wouldn't go running to her parents with tales of immoral behaviour and late nights. More like an uncle than a neighbour, Arthur was also a friend.

He enjoyed gardening, grew tomatoes and other vegetables in his greenhouse, and Emily had often helped him. Watering the plants, picking tomatoes, tending the grapevine he'd bought her for her fifth birthday; Emily had always got on well with him. If only she'd got on as well with her father, too. The grapevine had been nurtured and allowed to grow - unlike her.

But she was sure that Arthur would allow her to behave like a normal teenage girl for a couple of weeks - even if her parents wouldn't.

Wandering into the wine bar at seven o'clock Emily looked about her. People were laughing, joking, the chink of glasses blending with the music. A good-looking lad eyed her up and down and flashed her a cocky, lopsided grin. Feeling self-conscious, nervous, Emily tugged her short skirt down in a futile attempt to cover her thighs. She'd never been into a bar before, never tasted alcohol. This was a new and exciting experience for her.

'Hi,' Christine trilled, waving from her stool at the bar.

Again tugging her skirt ineffectually, Emily walked to her friend. 'This place is amazing,' she said, her lovely face beaming. Freedom was tasting good.

'It'll get busy later so grab yourself a barstool,' her best friend advised. 'You look great. I love your skirt.'

'It's not too short, is it?' Emily asked innocently.

'Don't be silly, it's perfect. Leather suits you. Drink?'

'Erm... orange juice, please. Do you like my new image?' Emily asked, desperate for her friend's approval. 'I must admit I feel rather self-conscious.'

'Of course you don't,' the girl giggled. 'You look fantastic, Emily. You look like a beautiful young woman rather than a...'

'A what? A frump?'

'No, I meant it's about time you got out and enjoyed yourself,' Christine said defensively.

'Yes, well, you know what my father's like.'

'Don't I just,' Christine scoffed. 'Anyway, your parents are away for two weeks so you can have some fun.'

'I suppose so,' Emily sighed.

'What is it? What's the matter?'

'My father has asked Arthur to keep an eye on me.'

'Arthur? Oh, your neighbour. He's okay, isn't he?'

'Yes, he's okay. It's just that... oh, I don't know. I might have guessed my parents wouldn't trust me.'

'Forget about them, Emily. You're free. Free to do as you like for a whole fortnight!'

Looking around the bar as Christine ordered the drinks, Emily tried not to think about her parents. Christine was right; she should forget about them and enjoy her freedom while it lasted. Sipping her drink, she let out a giggle as she imagined her father walking into the bar and staring at his little girl. Dressed in a miniskirt and tight blouse with make-up on... he'd disown her! Why did he treat her like a child? Would he ever allow her to grow up, to become an adult? She had to stop thinking about him, she knew, as the barman refilled her glass.

'This orange juice is nice,' she said. 'It tastes... I don't know. It tastes different.'

'I expect it does,' Christine laughed. 'It's vodka and orange.'

'Vodka?' Emily gasped. 'God, I shouldn't be—'

'Come on, Emily,' her friend quashed any protestations, 'chill out and enjoy yourself.'

'Yes, yes you're right,' Emily asserted. 'My parents are on holiday, and so am I.'

Gazing at Christine, Emily thought how attractive she was. With her black hair cascading over her naked shoulders and her dark eyes sparkling, she was a stunning girl. She was also very lucky. Her parents were normal, and allowed her to behave as a normal teenager. This would all be over in a couple of weeks, Emily thought dolefully. Her miniskirt and blouse would have to be hidden and she'd revert to the oppressed girl her parents knew and loved. But, she consoled herself, this was only day one - day one of fourteen.

'Why don't you move out?' Christine suggested. 'Move out and get your own flat.'

'I don't have any money,' Emily sighed. 'There's no way I could rent a flat. When I finish Uni and get a job I'll move out. But I can't afford to before then.'

'That's four years, Emily. You'll be twenty-two by then. God, four years of your parents...'

'I was trying to forget about my parents, if you remember?' Emily sulked.

'Sorry. Okay, let's have another round of drinks. Live for the moment, Emily. That's what I reckon.'

Emily began to realise just how sheltered her life had been as the music and laughter grew louder. She'd never known privacy, never had the space to grow and develop. Only a mile away from the university, she lived at home rather than the halls of residence. No boyfriends, no fun. There had been one boy, she reflected. She'd met him at Uni and really liked him. They'd gone to the local cinema together, and in the back row he'd put his arm around her shoulder. Eventually, almost accidentally, his hand moved slowly down and squeezed her breast, which she'd quite enjoyed...

'What do you think of that one?' Christine asked excitedly, breaking into Emily's reverie. 'Tight jeans, good-looking, good bum. What do you reckon?'

'He's all right,' Emily replied, trying not to catch the young man's eyes as he gazed at her.

'All right? I'll bet he knows how to make a girl happy.'

Emily turned away from the young man and gazed into her glass. She was a virgin, and felt uncomfortable talking like that. Downing another vodka and orange she felt dizzy rather than confident. She had hoped the alcohol would have brought her out of her shell, helped to loosen her up. Still a virgin at eighteen? Maybe after another drink or two...

'Alcohol always makes me feel horny,' Christine giggled. 'I wouldn't mind getting inside his boxer shorts!'

'Christine!' Emily breathed, her face flushing. 'He might hear you!'

'I hope he does,' her friend went on brazenly, 'I could do with a good fuck.'

Sipping her fresh drink, Emily realised she had a lot of catching up to do. Shy, naïve, nervous, self-conscious... hoping the lad wouldn't come over and chat to her she slumped her shoulders and lowered her head. She felt as though she was in the front row of a theatre, cowering in case the comedian dragged her onto the stage and made fun of her. There were several young men milling about in the bar, looking at her, eyeing her up and down. This was a stage, she mused. The men eyeing up the girls, thoughts of sex prominent in their male heads. But she had to admit that she rather liked the attention.

Swaying from side to side as she wandered up the path to her front door, Emily giggled. She'd thoroughly enjoyed the evening, had the time of her life. The lights, the music, too much vodka, the people. She felt as if she'd been to another world. Fumbling with her key, she finally managed to open the front door and stagger into the hall, where she gazed with bleary eyes at the stairs and imagined her father stomping down in his dressing gown, and thanked God he wasn't there to greet her as she swayed and almost fell over.

Her auburn hair dishevelled, she let out another giggle as she imagined his shocked expression as he stared in horror at her miniskirt, her tight blouse, and the teasingly exposed cleavage of her breasts. He'd accuse her of being a tart, send her to her room and ground her for a month or more. What had become of his darling daughter? But he was a thousand miles away in Spain, and none the wiser.

'What time do you call this?' Arthur suddenly demanded, pushing the unclosed front door open and stepping into the hall.

'Arthur,' Emily gasped, her wide eyes staring in horror at her neighbour. 'You made me jump.'

'Emily, it's half-past eleven,' he told her dourly.

'Is it?' She smirked as she tried to focus on her wrist. 'I can't even see my watch, let alone tell the time.'

'You'd better sit down before you fall down,' he ordered, taking her hand and leading her into the lounge. I dread to think what your father will say about this.'

'He won't know,' she slurred, flopping onto the sofa. 'Not unless you tell him.'

'Of course I'll tell him.' He was stern, his expression severe. 'I'm not going to lie to him, Emily.'

'You don't have to lie,' she said, wondering what he was getting at. 'Just don't mention it.'

'It amounts to the same thing,' he returned, fleetingly eyeing the triangular patch of her white panties as she reclined untidily on the sofa. She wasn't aware of the man's gaze, his hooded eyes locked to the delicate cotton snugly cosseting her full sex lips. Her head spinning with the effects of the alcohol, she was oblivious to her careless exhibitionism or his intense attention. With her skirt rising a little more as she slid down the sofa, she inadvertently parted her slender thighs and Arthur's eyes narrowed as he focused on the neat triangle of white cotton between her lovely limbs. In her miniskirt and tight blouse, Emily was an extremely enticing girl.

Unable to tear his eyes off her panties, Arthur moved a little closer. Emily's thighs lazily lolled a little further apart as she smoothed her auburn hair back with one hand and tried to focus on her looming neighbour. With the flimsy white material covering her sex barely wide enough to conceal the fleshy swell of her lips, the buttons of her blouse straining to contain the ripeness of her breasts, and her leather miniskirt riding higher up her thighs until it was almost little more than a belt, she held her hand to her head as the room span. Was Arthur really so angry with her for being a little late getting home? What was he thinking as he stared at her? Was he really going to tell on her to her parents?

'Look at the way you're dressed,' he said disapprovingly, dragging his eyes away from the delicate swell of her panties. 'You look like a... like a...'

'You sound just like my father,' she giggled, hauling herself upright and crossing her legs, her thighs whispering together in a way that drew Arthur's dark stare to them. 'What's the matter with the way I look?'

'This is serious, Emily,' he said. 'I'll have to note this in the report book.'

'Report book?' she echoed, sobering up as she realised he *was* serious.

'Your parents left at six, and three quarters of an hour later you went out dressed like a... like a tart. You then come home drunk at eleven-thirty. Your mother specifically said she wanted you home by ten.'

'Arthur, I'm not drunk,' Emily said, suddenly feeling uneasy about him and his mood.

'Your parents trusted you, Emily. And this is how you repay them.'

'It's hardly late,' she countered. 'I'm eighteen, Arthur. I'm an adult, not a child.'

'It doesn't matter how old you are. This is your parents' house, and you have to abide by their rules while you're living here. Now, you'd better get to bed. We'll discuss this further tomorrow.'

Waiting until she heard the front door close, Emily dragged herself up from the sofa and climbed the stairs. This had been the last thing she'd expected. Collapsing on her bed, she lay on her back and watched the ceiling spinning round, wishing she'd not drunk all that vodka. What was the matter with Arthur? What had come over him? He needed to chill out a bit. A report book? What crap. She was eighteen and a university student, not a schoolgirl. With her eyes drifting closed, she hoped this was just a bad dream as she fell asleep.

The morning came all too quickly. Her head pounding, her miniskirt rucked up around her hips, Emily sat upright and looked around her bedroom. Thoughts of Arthur filtering into her mind as sleep left her, she knew she'd not been dreaming. Realising that he must have been looking out for her, waiting for her to come home, she couldn't understand his attitude. He was supposed to be keeping an eye on her, not behaving like a Victorian schoolmaster.

Taking a shower, Emily knew she was going to have to talk to him. Perhaps he'd been in a bad mood and took it out on her. A report book? Sure that he hadn't been serious as she stepped out of the shower and wrapped a towel around her curvaceous body, she thought back a few years. Arthur had once told her not to worry when her parents forbade her to wear a short skirt. He'd chatted to her, listened and understood. He'd often taken her aside and explained that she wouldn't always be under the restrictions of her parents. So why the sudden change now?

Slipping into her bra and knickers, she sat at her dressing table and dried her hair. At least the university had broken up for the summer. She couldn't have faced lectures on business studies with her head aching like it was. And she felt nauseous, too. Deciding to have a quiet day before going out with Christine again that evening, she knew she was going to have to be careful. Perhaps she should leave the house by the backdoor and sneak down the path to the alleyway. Arthur's office was upstairs at the front of his house, overlooking the street. He'd not be watching from the back windows.

Hearing the doorbell, she slipped into her dressing gown and went downstairs. Reckoning that Christine had called round for a coffee and a chat, she was surprised to find Arthur standing on the porch step. He'd come to apologise, she was sure as she invited him in and offered to put the kettle on. She reckoned he'd thought about the previous evening and realised he'd gone over the top.

'About last night,' he began. Was there an apology in his expression?

'I *was* rather late,' she acknowledged, plugging in the kettle and taking two cups from the cupboard. 'I got talking to Christine, and—'

'I know how it is,' he interrupted her. 'Chatting with a friend, enjoying a few drinks, the time just flies by.'

'I had every intention of getting home by ten,' she said with some relief.

'I'm sure you did, but, the thing is—'

'I won't be late again,' she hurriedly insisted. 'There's no need to worry about that.'

'I hope not, Emily,' he said, nodding pensively. 'You see, I feel responsible for you. Your parents asked me to keep an eye on you, and so...'

'I know, Arthur. I'm sorry, okay? I've been a naughty girl and I won't do it again.' Her dressing gown parting as she bent a little, revealing the alluring cleavage of her young breasts, Emily took the milk from the fridge. She thought nothing of wearing her dressing gown in front of her neighbour. Despite giving a glimpse of her bra cups and the front of her tight panties, she felt perfectly comfortable with Arthur and thought nothing of it. He was a family friend, almost an uncle figure. He wouldn't even notice such things...

'To be honest,' he sighed, sipping his coffee as she replaced the milk and pulled her gown together, 'I wish your parents hadn't involved me.'

'So do I,' Emily said, forcing a laugh. 'I'm perfectly all right on my own. After all it's only for a couple of weeks, so what's the worst that can happen? Anyway, what's this report book you mentioned?'

'That was your father's idea. He wants to know what time you go out, what time you get home each evening, and—'

'So there really is a report book?' Emily gasped.

'Yes, there is. The problem I have is that I can't lie to him. I can't leave a blank space in the book because he'll ask me about it. And if for last night I write ten o'clock in the getting home column, I'd be lying, wouldn't I?'

'This is ridiculous,' Emily complained, her gown parting again as she shook her head in disbelief. 'A report book? The "getting home" column?'

'You, of all people, should know what your father is like,' Arthur pointed out.

'Yes, but all you have to say is that you didn't see me come home. Surely he doesn't expect you to be spying out of the window all night?'

'He trusts me, Emily. I've known your parents since you were knee-high to a grasshopper. They asked me to keep an eye on you and the house because they trust me.'

'Then I'll be in by ten this evening, I promise,' she stated adamantly, seeing appeasement as her best move.

'You're going out?' He focused on the smooth plateau of her stomach, the small indent of her navel. 'You're going out again?'

She nodded, oblivious to his scrutiny. 'I'm meeting Christine.'

'I'd rather you didn't, Emily.'

'What do you mean?'

'You'll stay in this evening. Do you understand me?'

'What?' she gasped, frowning at him. Had she misheard him? 'You mean, you're grounding me?'

'Yes, I am,' he confirmed matter-of-factly. 'I'll feel a lot better if I punish you.'

Her mouth fell open. 'Punish me? Arthur, this is crazy.'

'I'll cover for you, this one time. I'll fill in the report book - and this really goes against the grain - and I'll say you were home by ten last night.'

'Right, thanks,' Emily breathed, sensing she didn't really know her neighbour at all. What on earth was the matter with him?

'But your punishment will be that you'll stay home this evening. I don't like this any more than you do. I'm taking quite a risk for you, Emily.'

'A risk?' she repeated incredulously. 'How do you mean, a risk?'

'Well, what if one of the other neighbours saw you last night and told your parents that you got home at eleven-thirty... you can understand my predicament, can't you?'

Emily suddenly felt humbled, and lowered her eyes from his accusatory glare. 'Yes, yes I suppose I can,' she acknowledged.

'If your parents discovered that I'd covered for you, lied for you...'

'Look, I won't be late again, I promise.' She needed to placate him.

'All right, but as I say, you'll stay in this evening by way of punishment,' he insisted uncompromisingly.

The minute Arthur had finished his coffee and left the house Emily rang Christine, who couldn't believe it any more than Emily could. A report book? Grounded by her next-door neighbour? Suggesting that Emily sneak out of the house once dusk fell, Christine said she'd meet her in the wine bar and from there they'd go on to a club she knew. Music, drinking, dancing, boys; they'd have a great time - and Emily anxiously bit her lip as she agreed to the irresistible plan. This was a dangerous game, she knew. Her holiday in Tenerife was riding on her behaviour, and if she blew things she could forget it.

Chapter 2

Emily waited until nine o'clock before slipping out of the backdoor and making her escape. Arthur wouldn't have spotted her sneaking into the alleyway, she was certain. He'd probably been looking out of his office window at the front, watching the street. Having grounded her, it was unlikely he'd expect her to creep out of the house. And if he called round to check on her, he'd think she'd not answered the doorbell because she'd had an early night. Or was she overreacting?

She had a great evening with Christine, behaving like any normal eighteen-year-old girl. Meeting several of her university friends in the nightclub she giggled and joked, really coming out of herself. Briefly reflecting on her teenage years, she knew she'd missed out on a lot. While her friends had been partying and going out with boys she'd been studying at home and going to bed by ten. But things were different now - at least for a while.

When she returned home she crept in through the backdoor and breathed a sigh of relief. The lights were off in Arthur's house. It was almost two o'clock and he'd be tucked up in his bed, oblivious to her transgression. Making herself a cup of coffee, her head again dizzy with the effect of alcohol, she pondered her evening with Chrissie.

The nightclub had been amazing, the drinks flowed and she finally built up the courage to dance with a lad. She'd not told Christine, but she arranged to meet him in the wine bar the following evening. His name was Jack and he was great company. He made her laugh and bought her drinks, and treated her like the young woman she was. Her stomach somersaulting she recalled his lips touching hers, and incredible though it was, that was her first ever kiss.

'I'm in here,' Arthur's voice broke the night's silence, coming from the lounge, and Emily almost dropped her mug as she spun round and stared into the darkness of the hall. The lounge light came on and Arthur called out again. She glanced at the kitchen clock. Five past two. This wasn't happening, it couldn't be. How the hell had he got in? She'd locked the doors, for certain. Her hands trembling, her heart racing, she placed her mug on the kitchen table and ventured along the hall to the lounge.

'You defied me, Emily,' he said, looking up at her from the armchair.

'What - what are you doing here?' she stammered, her brown eyes reflecting fear as she stared at him.

'Waiting for you,' he replied. He gazed at her leather miniskirt and shook his head disapprovingly. 'It's past two o'clock, Emily. Not only are you four hours late, but you shouldn't have gone out in the first place. What have you to say for yourself?'

'This is silly,' she said, wondering what had happened to the friendly neighbour she once knew. 'This is... it's silly.'

'Silly? That's not the word I'd use. It's despicable. What are your parents going to say?' He locked his dark eyes to hers and scowled. 'The day they go away you come home drunk at eleven-thirty. The very next day, even though you were grounded you come rolling in at two o'clock, drunk again.'

'I'm not drunk.'

'Look at you. You can hardly stand. Have you been with a boy?'

'A boy?' she echoed, feeling like a naughty schoolgirl as she twisted her auburn locks nervously around her slender fingers.

'Yes, a boy.'

'No, I... I was with Christine.'

'I don't believe that for one minute. You've been with a boy, haven't you?'

'No, I—'

'Don't lie to me, Emily,' he broke in angrily and lowered his gaze to her shapely thighs, revealed by her miniskirt. 'You're dressed like a young tart,' he said harshly. 'Had some young lout's hands down your panties, have you?'

'Of course not!' she shrieked, unable to believe what he was suggesting. 'For goodness sake, I've only been out with Christine.'

'Is that why you're so late?' he pressed. 'Because you've been in the park allowing some yob to—'

'Arthur, please, I have *not* been out with a lad, let alone let one touch me where you're suggesting!' she retorted indignantly. 'And even if I had it would have nothing to do with you. I'm eighteen, I can do as I please—'

'You don't seem to understand the situation, Emily,' he interrupted. 'During your parents' absence I am responsible for you.'

'How did you get into my house?' she demanded, trying to think straight.

'You mean your *parents'* house,' he corrected pettily. 'I let myself in with a key. Your father gave it to me before they left.'

'So you think you can come walking in here as if you own the place and—'

'This is getting tedious, Emily. You have behaved despicably, and I now have to decide on your punishment.'

'Punishment?' She held her hand to her head as she tried to comprehend the ridiculous situation. 'I want you to go now,' she said. 'I'm tired and I want you to leave so I can go to bed.'

'You still don't understand, do you?' he said, shaking his head. 'Allow me to explain. You want to go on holiday with Christine later this year, and as your father said, this is a test period. Are you with me so far?'

'Yes,' Emily sighed, raising her eyes to the ceiling.

'Whether or not you go to Tenerife depends on me. It depends on the report I give your parents. I've not yet filled in the time you got home last night or tonight, but eleven-thirty and gone two o'clock won't look good. And not only drunk on both occasions, but dressed like a young tart, too.'

'You can't speak to me like that,' Emily protested, failing to suppress her anger. 'Who do you think you are?'

'Oh, I omitted to mention that there's a remarks column in the report book so I can comment on specific examples of bad behaviour. Again, it was your father's idea. Now, why don't you make me a cup of coffee while I decide what to do with you?'

Leaving the lounge sulkily, Emily knew he held the key to her holiday. Did it really mean that much to her? Yes, it did. It wasn't just that she was going to Tenerife; after the excitement of the wine bar and the nightclub, she was looking forward to going away with Christine more than ever. Tenerife meant freedom, fun, music, dancing. She'd do anything to be allowed to go on holiday.

But what had happened to change Arthur like this? Why had he turned into a Victorian-like guardian? She was determined not to be dictated to by her suddenly draconian next-door neighbour. To keep a neighbourly eye on the house - and on her - was understandable and kind of him. But to question her and suggest what he'd suggested? No, he wasn't going to rule her life for the next two minutes, let alone two weeks.

'Thanks,' he said, smiling as Emily went back to the lounge and gave him his coffee. 'When I was a boy my father was pretty strict. He'd take the slipper to me if I misbehaved, and it didn't do me any harm. In fact, it taught me to respect him.'

'That's when you were a boy,' Emily said. 'Not when you were eighteen, surely?'

'By the time I'd reached eighteen I'd learned to behave myself, learned to respect my parents. Can't you see that yours merely want the best for you? They don't want to have to worry about you while they're in Spain. They don't want to be wondering what you're up to, where you've been, what time you're getting home. What if something happened to you?'

'I realise they're concerned about me, but,' feeling suddenly dizzy Emily sat on the sofa. 'We used to talk, Arthur,' she sighed. 'Many times you'd listen to my problems—'

'You're living under your parents' roof and under their rule,' he interrupted brusquely, and brushing her auburn hair away from her pretty face she tried to clear her mind. She couldn't understand what had happened to Arthur, why he'd changed. They used to sit in his garden beneath the summer sun, talking about the plants, school, anything and everything.

Reclining on the sofa, her leather miniskirt riding up her smooth thighs, she was unaware that her white knickers were on show. Arthur stared at her from the armchair, his dark eyes locked to the triangular patch of material clinging to the fleshy cushions of her teenage love lips. The alluring V-shape of her panties perfectly visible beneath her miniskirt as she unconsciously allowed her thighs to fall apart, she was oblivious to her exhibitionism.

'As I said, you have behaved despicably,' Arthur stated sternly. 'And as to your punishment...'

'You're not going to suggest that you take the slipper to me, are you?' Emily asked him sarcastically, sitting upright.

'I believe that a spanking might make you change your ways, Emily, yes,' he announced, making her wish she'd not been so flippant.

'A spanking?' she gasped. 'Now hang on just one minute—'

'You still don't realise the gravity of the situation, do you?' he cut in. 'You don't seem to comprehend the severity of your predicament.'

'Gravity? Severity? All I did was—'

'All you did was go against everything your parents stand for. And, like it or not, that is a grave lack of respect.'

'You can't spank me,' she muttered, forcing a laugh as her firm buttocks involuntarily tensed. 'I'm eighteen years old and I won't allow you to.'

'Don't defy me, young lady,' he warned fiercely. 'Perhaps you should have been spanked when you were younger; you might not have found yourself in this situation had you received discipline from an early age. Now bend over the back of that chair,' he added, nodding at the other armchair.

'What?' she gasped disbelievingly. 'You're not serious, surely?'

'I've never been more serious,' he returned, rising to his feet and pulling the armchair into the centre of the room. 'Bend over the back of it, Emily.'

'No, I won't,' she said adamantly.

'Dressed like a common tart, answering back to your betters, coming home at two in the morning so drunk you can hardly stand,' he growled. 'You can forget Tenerife.'

Staring at her neighbour, Emily felt her heart beating violently. This was ridiculous. Her father was strict and had given her the odd whack on the bum when she deserved it, but he'd never told her to bend over the back of a chair. She didn't understand what had come over Arthur, but why he'd changed didn't matter, she concluded. The point was that her holiday was hanging in the balance. Arthur knew as well as she did that a bad report would put an end to her plans of going abroad with Christine.

'Well?' he said, eyeing the shadowy cleavage between her breasts. 'The choice is yours, Emily. You either take your punishment from me or your father. Which is it to be?'

'This is blackmail,' she sulked, raising her trembling body from the sofa.

'Blackmail? Don't be ridiculous. This is discipline. You're obviously not used to discipline.'

'Not used to it?' she scoffed. 'All I've had is years of discipline.'

'In that case it's done you no good whatsoever,' he retorted disdainfully. 'Your behaviour thus far has been extremely poor, so now you're to be punished. Bend over as I told you to.'

Standing behind the armchair, Emily knew she had no choice. If her father read the report book that would be the end of her holiday chances, but if she went along with Arthur, allowed him to spank her, then she might be allowed to go to Tenerife.

Finally bending over the upholstered back and placing her hands flat on the seat, her short skirt rising up her thighs, exposing the tight material of her white panties, she closed her eyes and waited with dread. Arthur stood behind her, and it was all incredibly humiliating.

The first smack from the man's palm across the tensed globes of her buttocks jolted her young body and she let out a yelp. The second slap was harder, the stinging sensation permeating the sensitive flesh of her rounded bottom. Biting her lip she thought it might be best not to go out at night. Jeopardising her holiday wasn't worth it, so it might be best to stay in for the next two weeks. 'No,' she protested as Arthur lifted her short skirt up onto her lower back.

'I'm a lenient man,' he stated, his palm meeting the tight cotton cosseting her teenage bottom with a loud slap, 'but perhaps I should have spanked you years ago.'

'Please, that's enough,' she begged.

'Let this be a lesson to you, young lady,' he said, as though not hearing her plea, administering the hardest slap yet.

'Please, I...'

'Look at your excuse for a skirt. You're nothing but a shameless tart; drinking, answering back at me; you should be ashamed of yourself.'

Again and again he spanked the cotton-covered orbs of her burning bottom as she squirmed and writhed over the back of the armchair. Her protests only firing his anger, he pinned her down with his free hand on the middle of her back as he continued the merciless spanking of her bottom. Even her father wouldn't do this. As strict as he was he'd never hold her down forcefully and spank her. Her breathing fast and shallow, tears welling in her eyes, she prayed for her sadistic neighbour to leave her alone as he finally halted the gruelling punishment. She never wanted to see him again, never wanted to speak to him again.

Hauling her trembling body upright as he moved aside, Emily smoothed her skirt down to conceal her panties. Her pretty face flushed, she winced as she rubbed her stinging buttocks through the tight material of the short garment. Arthur was crazy, she decided, watching him sip his coffee. The man was a lunatic. Was he possessed?

'You'll stay in tomorrow night.' he calmly ordered, finishing his coffee. 'Do you understand me?'

'Yes,' she murmured, hanging her head as a tear rolled down her cheek.

'I don't like this any more than you do, Emily,' he said. 'But as I'm responsible for your welfare I won't tolerate any nonsense. Now, you'd better get yourself to bed.'

He left the house and Emily flinched as the front door closed. Even though her buttocks stung like hell, a poignant reminder of her punishment, she still couldn't believe what had happened. The humiliation had been unbearable. He'd seen her panties and spanked her buttocks. She could have stopped him, she reflected as she wearily climbed the stairs to her bedroom. She could have told him to sod off. But that would definitely have put paid to her holiday.

Her thoughts turning to the young man she'd arranged to meet the following evening, she wondered what to do. If she slipped out of the backdoor again Arthur would see her, she had no doubt about that now. He'd be lurking. She daren't risk going to the wine bar.

Even if she talked Arthur into allowing her out she'd have to be home by ten o'clock, so what would she say to Jack? She'd arranged to meet him at eight; she could hardly tell him she had to be home again by ten. There was no point in meeting him. She might as well forget about it.

Waking to the sun streaming through her bedroom window the following morning, Emily hauled her tired self out of bed and stood before the mirror. Turning, she lifted her nightdress and focused on the crimsoned globes of her naked buttocks. This was a nightmare, she thought, imaging Arthur appearing in the doorway to check up on her. With a feeling of oppression engulfing her, she was afraid to take a shower in case he let himself into the house and came looking for her. Did she have no privacy?

Convinced he'd lost his senses, she slipped into the bathroom and locked the door. But stepping into the shower she couldn't help thinking he'd knock and ask what she was up to. Feeling like a prisoner in her own home as she lathered shampoo into her auburn locks, she realised she had to calm down and stop worrying. Arthur wouldn't come into the house to check up on her, would he? He wouldn't knock on the bathroom door.

Turning off the shower and wrapping a towel around her naked body, she listened at the door before unlocking it. She was safe, she was sure as she padded across the landing to her bedroom. Deciding to go down and slip the catch up on the front door, she wondered why she'd not thought of it earlier. Then even though Arthur had a key he'd be locked out. Again eyeing the crimsoned flesh of her naked buttocks in the mirror, she tugged her panties up her shapely legs and concealed the evidence of the gruelling spanking. But she'd pushed all thoughts of her parents to the back of her mind, and now she was going to forget about Arthur, too.

Munching tasty marmalade on toast for breakfast, Emily looked out of the kitchen window at the garden. It was a beautiful summer morning, lovely for sunbathing. She'd bought a bikini for Tenerife, but dare she wear it now? No one overlooked the patio, no one would see her if she slipped into her bikini and soaked up the sun. It would be nice to get a bit of a tan in readiness for her holiday.

Quickly finishing her toast and coffee, she dashed up to her bedroom and slipped her T-shirt and bra off. Then tugging her skirt and panties down she slipped into her new bikini. Again looking at her reflection in the mirror, she grinned. The turquoise two-piece fitted well, accentuating the fullness of her young breasts and the toned roundness of her buttocks, although the panties were rather tight, moulding to the gentle swell of her pubic curls at the front.

Grabbing a towel from the airing cupboard, she hurried nimbly back downstairs. Knowing Arthur wouldn't be able to see her from his house or garden, she felt safe as she wandered out to the patio. This was freedom, she mused, the sun warming her creamy skin as she looked up at the cloudless sky. This was what normal teenage girls would do, enjoying sunbathing in a bikini.

Spreading the towel out on a lounger she lay on her back and closed her eyes. She could never have sunbathed in a bikini with her parents around. Her father would have said that sunbathing was not only unnecessary, but also unhealthy. Even in Spain her parents would remain fully clothed and in the shade. If her father knew she was wearing a skimpy bikini and lying beneath the sun on their patio... but he was many, many miles away.

Tenerife was going to be great, she thought, the sun warming her flesh and muscles deliciously. Relaxing on the beach with Chrissie, drinking in the bars and dancing the night away in the clubs, really enjoying life. No one was going to ruin her holiday. Not her parents, not Arthur - no one.

'What on earth do you think you're doing?' Arthur demanded, standing over Emily's scantily clad form.

'Oh, I - I,' she stammered, sitting bolt upright and folding her arms to conceal the tight material of her bikini straining to contain her breasts. 'H-how did you...?'

'This is the real you, isn't it? he said scathingly. 'Lying nearly naked in the garden. My God, your parents went very wrong with your upbringing.'

'I'm not nearly naked,' she objected. 'I'm only enjoying a little sunbathing—'

'The minute they go away you behave like a little tart. And that's just what you are, young lady. You're a little tart. Get into the house this instant.'

'Wait a minute,' she snapped, looking up at him silhouetted against the bright sun. 'Get out of my garden. How dare you come round here and—?'

'Is there no end to your shameless behaviour?' he snapped. 'I'll tell you this, my girl; unless you get into the house now I'll add a few more entries in the report book.'

'What... what do you mean?' she asked fearfully. 'Surely you wouldn't deliberately get me into trouble by making things up?'

'Let's just say I'm not prepared to tolerate this sort of behaviour, Emily,' he said ambiguously. 'Now get inside.'

Rising to her feet, Emily grabbed the towel and wrapped it around her body. Arthur followed her into the kitchen and closed the backdoor, his dark eyes scowling as he ordered her to go into the lounge. Dressed only in her bikini she held the towel tightly around her torso, and feeling his stare on the crotch of her bikini, she wished it were larger. Emily cringed with embarrassment, but she was sure he wouldn't dare touch her. Physical discipline was one thing, but to spank her in just a bikini? He wouldn't dare.

Cringing as he again ordered her to go through to the lounge she felt her heart racing, pumping adrenalin through her veins. She'd only been sunbathing, she thought anxiously, walking into the lounge with her neighbour in tow. It wasn't a crime to sunbathe in the privacy of her own back garden. What had happened to change the man so much?

'Bend over,' he ordered, again dragging the armchair into the centre of the room.

'Arthur, please,' she whispered.

'Please? Please what?'

'Please, be sensible about this,' she expanded. 'I'm only wearing my bikini; it isn't proper. What do you think my father would say if he knew you'd spanked me over his favourite armchair, and with me in only a bikini?'

'Are you threatening me, young lady?'

'No, all I'm saying is that this isn't looking out for me, this is—'

'Yes?'

'It's... he won't believe you,' she said triumphantly. 'He knows I never sunbathe in the garden, let alone own a bikini. There's no way my father will believe you.'

'I see,' he reflected. 'So you intend to tell him I'm a liar?'

'Yes, if I have to,' she said defiantly.

'Hm, this really does change things,' he sighed.

'I - I didn't want it to be like this,' she said apologetically, sensing him backing down, that she'd won the day. 'But what with the way you've been treating me, I have no choice other than to tell my parents that any bad things you report about my behaviour is a lie.'

'I was afraid something like this might happen,' he said.

'Just leave me alone and I'll not mention any of this to them,' she said in conciliatory tones.

'Mention any of what, Emily?' he quizzed, frowning as though deeply puzzled, but continued before she could answer. 'That sounds like a threat to me. As I said, I was afraid something like this might happen. As you know I work with computers, and I have a digital camera. And now I also have several shots of you brazenly flaunting yourself on the patio.'

'So?' she challenged, trying to hide her shock at hearing her neighbour had actually taken sneaky shots of her.

'Sunbathing in a bikini?' he sneered. 'I know exactly what he'll do. And I have other photographs, Emily. I have several of you leaving the house dressed like a tart.'

'I don't believe you,' she said stubbornly, despite secretly believing him capable of anything by now.

'If you'd like to come round to my house I'll show you,' he said casually. 'I'll even print some copies for you.

'Now I want you to stop this nonsense, Emily,' he went on, seizing back the initiative. 'You're making my life very difficult. Your parents entrusted me to keep an eye on you, and you're doing your best to make my job impossible.'

'And you're doing your best to take advantage of the situation, to take advantage of me,' she accused.

'What are you implying, young lady?'

'You know every well what I'm talking about. This is a sexual thing, isn't it?'

'A sexual thing?' he said, aghast. 'How dare you suggest that I...? Pull your bikini bottoms down and bend over the back of the chair.'

'Pull my...?' Emily shook her head in denial. 'No, no I won't.'

'Emily, unless you—'

'Who on earth do you think you are?' the confused girl shrieked, her anger exploding.

'Do you want your parents to discover the truth about their sweet little daughter? Do you want me to tell them how you've behaved behind their backs?'

Holding the towel over her breasts, Emily couldn't understand why Arthur had taken photographs of her sunbathing on the patio. What was he trying to do? He seemed to be building evidence against her, compiling a dossier. But why? This was only day three of fourteen days - day three of a horrendous nightmare. Was she going to have to stay in the house day in, day out? Whatever he was up to, she couldn't really believe it was something sexual. No, he wasn't like that. And he was over fifty.

'I've often wondered why your parents haven't been stricter with you,' he said, pointing to the back of the chair.

'Stricter?' she said. 'God, I'm hardly allowed to breathe when they're around.'

'But it hasn't worked, has it? Now pull your bikini bottoms down and bend over, young lady. The more you defy me the harder it will be for you.'

'I'm not going to allow you to touch me,' she insisted. 'If my parents knew what you're up to they'd never speak to you again.'

'There's more to this than you realise,' he said enigmatically. 'For a few years I've known you've been going off the rails. You lie to your parents, and I don't like that.'

'Lie to them?' she said resentfully. 'I've never lied to them.'

'I first caught you out last year. You told your father you were going to Christine's house for an evening to study. I was here when you told him.'

'So, what's wrong with that?'

'You didn't go to Christine's house, that's what's wrong. You went to the park with her.'

'You followed me?'

'For your own good, yes, I did. You met two lads there, didn't you?'

'Yes, I remember it,' she admitted. 'We bumped into a couple of lads from Uni, that was all.'

'You know that, and I know that,' he conceded. 'But if I told your parents that you and your friend got up to immoral things with those young louts...'

'You're mad,' Emily gasped. 'Why say something like that? Why do you want me to get into trouble with my parents?'

'I don't. That's why I'm taking charge of you. From now on you'll answer to me; you'll do exactly as I say without protesting or arguing. I'm determined to discipline you, Emily. Now, pull your bikini down and bend over the back of the chair.'

Leaving her bikini in place and still holding the towel tightly around her, Emily, defeated and reluctant, leaned over the back of the chair and tensed the smooth globes of her buttocks as Arthur stood behind her. She knew that even if she stayed in every night he would give her parents a bad report of her. What did he want from her? *Was* this a sexual thing? The man she'd thought she'd come to know so well, the man who was more like an uncle than a neighbour, was his mind brimming with thoughts of a sexual nature?

There was no way out of this, she knew as he ran his fingertips over the tight material of her bikini bottoms, teasing the pert spheres of her buttocks. Humiliation engulfed her. She'd never felt so embarrassed in her life. Her bottom presented, displayed to her neighbour like this was degradation in the extreme. Not only was her holiday in serious jeopardy, but also her father would ground her for months once he'd listened to Arthur's lies. This was a nightmare!

The first slap jolting her young body, she squeezed her eyes shut and did her best not to protest. Once her parents were home Arthur wouldn't be able to touch her. If she could just endure this for a couple of weeks, or better still stay in every night and be on her best behaviour to thwart him. But she now feared that whether she stayed in every night or not, Arthur would dream up some reason or other to spank her. As the second slap landed squarely across her bikini, stinging the tensed flesh of her bottom, she wondered if he'd been planning all this for some time. Had he been waiting for an opportunity to get his hands on her and live out some perverse fantasy?

'That'll be enough for now,' he announced, having stung her poor bottom with a third slap that resounded around the comfortable lounge. 'Three should be enough to give you a taste of what you'll get if you misbehave again.'

'I'll be staying in every night from now on,' she whispered contritely, straightening up and still holding the towel tightly around herself with one hand, whilst ruefully rubbing her buttocks with the other. 'I'll not leave the house until my parents get back.'

'I'm pleased to hear it, Emily,' he smiled. 'You see, the punishment has worked.'

'No, it hasn't. I'm not staying in because of the spanking. I'm staying in so you'll have no reason to come round here again.'

'Good, I won't have to worry about you then,' he said amiably. 'In fact, I'll be able to get on with my work uninterrupted.'

'I know your game,' she said, cupping one stinging buttock. 'You planned this. You were waiting until my parents went away so you could—'

'Be careful what you say, young lady,' he warned. 'Irresponsible talk can get people into trouble. All I want is what's best for you. I merely want to see you remain a respectable young lady, not a young tart who drinks alcohol and answers back to her betters and disobeys authority.'

'I do not—'

'The day will come when you'll meet a nice young man and settle down,' he continued as though she wasn't talking. 'Then you'll thank me for disciplining you. I can promise you that.'

'Thank you?' she scoffed, pulling the towel tighter around her shapely bosom. 'You must be joking. I've never known anyone like you. You're an evil man, and I don't like you any more.'

'I can understand why you think that,' he acknowledged with infuriating calm. 'But you will thank me one day.'

'No, I'll hate you for the rest of my life,' she vowed.

'Emily, what would your parents say if they were to see a photograph of you bending over the back of your father's favourite armchair?'

'I beg your pardon?' Emily's lovely eyes widened in disbelief.

'I have my camera in my pocket,' he told her. 'I took a photograph of you while you were bending over and distracted. So if I tell your parents that I saw a young man leaving their house one morning, if I say he dropped something on the path and I went out to pick it up... well, what would they say if they discovered you'd invited a randy yob back here, let alone allowed him to take a photograph of you half-naked and bending over the back of the chair while indulging in some perverted sexual game?'

'Get out,' Emily hissed. 'Get out and stay out!'

'I will, Emily, I will. Just remember that you are now beholden to me. I'll correct your wicked ways if it's the last thing I do. I'll make a respectable, obedient young lady out of you no matter what it takes. And don't you dare defy me again by going out this evening. Hopefully you've learned your lesson on that score.'

As he left Emily curled up on the sofa and cried. He was an evil monster. He'd blackmailed her, betrayed her, and this was only day three. Had he taken photographs of her sunbathing and bending over the chair? If he had, and he showed them to her parents, her life wouldn't be worth living.

Chapter 3

Discovering an envelope containing several photographs on the doormat that afternoon, Emily held her hand to her head. Arthur hadn't been lying. First gazing at a shot of her bent over the armchair, she flicked through the further incriminating evidence of her sunbathing in a skimpy bikini. There were even shots of her leaving for the wine bar, in her tight blouse and miniskirt! Clutching the despicable photographs as she dashed into the hall to answer the phone, she hoped her parents weren't calling to see how she was. What could she say?

'Get the piccies?' Arthur asked as she pressed the receiver to her ear. 'They've turned out rather well, don't you agree?'

'What do you want from me?' she asked desperately, dreading his reply.

'I'll be round to talk to you in a minute,' he stated coldly. 'Why don't you put the kettle on? We'll have a nice chat over a cup of coffee.'

'Go to hell,' she snapped, slamming the phone down.

Hiding the photographs beneath the sofa she wondered what to do. She'd had a shower and had been getting ready to slip out again for the evening, but now? Pulling her dressing gown together and checking the time, she was determined to meet Jack in the wine bar as arranged. It was five in the afternoon - only three hours to go. This was a date she didn't want to miss, but with Arthur around, watching her every move...

Was she in for another spanking for some unjust reason? She wouldn't let him in, she decided, dashing into the hall and slipping the catch on the front door. He could ring the bell, threaten her, blackmail her, but there was no way she was going to allow him into the house ever again. If only she'd gone to Spain with her parents, after all.

Hearing a noise in the kitchen she froze. The backdoor was locked, she was sure. She'd locked it before taking her shower. Pulling her dressing gown together to conceal her lacy white bra, she felt the hairs on the back of her neck rising as she definitely heard the backdoor close. Someone was in the kitchen. Had the man a key to the back of the house too?

'Ah, there you are,' Arthur said, appearing in the hall from the kitchen.

'H-how did you...?' Emily stammered, staring in disbelief at her arrogant neighbour.

'I also have a key to the backdoor,' he confirmed her fears. 'Your father thought it a good idea.'

'Get out!' Emily shrieked. 'My God, you've got a nerve! Get out of this house, or I'll call the police.'

'There's no need to be like that,' he said, smiling at her. 'I've come round to have a friendly chat with you, that's all. We need to talk, Emily.'

'There's nothing to talk about.'

'Isn't there? I would have thought there's plenty to talk about.' Guiding her easily into the lounge and sitting on the sofa, he looked up at her as she moved back to the door. 'Don't go, Emily,' he said sternly. 'We're going to have a chat whether you like it or not. Please, sit down.'

'I don't want to have a chat,' she complained, sitting stiffly on the front edge of the armchair that had collaborated in her spankings.

'We've got off to a pretty bad start and I'd like to put things right,' he said.

'There's no way you can put things right,' she sulked, pouting. 'After what you've done to me there's nothing you can say or do to put things right.'

'I've known for some time that you've been in need of better disciplining, Emily,' he told her, 'in need of tighter control and a firmer hand than your parents give you.'

'No, you're just a sad pervert,' she said. 'You just want to—'

'I'm sorry to hear you say such a thing,' he cut in. 'I'm sorry because you insult me when all I'm trying to do is make a better person of you. You accused me of planning this, and that hurt, young lady. All I was hoping was that you'd behave and there'd be no need to punish you, but as things have turned out you've disappointed me.'

'I don't care whether you're disappointed or not,' she said defiantly, unmoved by his apparent disillusionment. 'As far as I'm concerned you have nothing to do with me. You're not my father. You're not even a relative. Now get out of this house.'

'You're not understanding me, are you?' he said smoothly. 'You're not listening, Emily.'

'Oh, I understand you only too well,' she countered.

He sighed. 'I didn't want to have to do this, but you've left me no choice.'

'Do what?'

'I'm going to teach you, Emily. I'm going to discipline you and teach you right from wrong, teach you to respect your betters.'

'You'll teach me nothing,' she asserted. 'Now get out of my house. Just get out.'

'I really didn't want to have to do this,' he went on, unflustered. 'The photograph of you sunbathing on the patio; I manipulated it on my computer. Using the airbrush I removed your bikini top. What will your parents say when they see you sunbathing topless on their patio?'

'I... I don't believe you,' she faltered, because deep down she did believe him completely.

'And although I say it myself I've done a very good job,' he said smugly. They say photographs don't lie...' He paused, his dark eyes looking her up and down as though he'd only just realised something. 'Why are you in your dressing gown at this time of day? Why is your hair camp?'

'I, um, I've just taken a shower,' she answered, pulling her gown tighter together. 'That is all right, isn't it? I mean, it's not against your rules to have a shower?'

'Were you planning to go out this evening?'

'No, I was just...'

'You were, weren't you? You were getting ready to go out despite my grounding you.'

'I was hot and took a shower, that's all,' she insisted unconvincingly.

'Take your dressing gown off,' he ordered, unmoved by her assurance. 'I'll teach you obedience if it's the last thing I do. Take it off this instant.'

'No, I don't care how much you threaten me,' she said rebelliously, 'I'll not—'

'Take your dressing gown off and place your hands flat on the coffee table,' he ordered.

'Why are you doing this to me, Arthur?' she pleaded.

'To discipline you,' he stated. 'It's as simple as that.'

'Why do you want to spank me again? What's your excuse this time?'

'Excuse? Don't you mean *reason?*'

'Your excuse or reason is that you're getting some sort of weird kick out of spanking me and being horrible to me.'

'No, I'll tell you the *reason*, Emily. I'm not being horrible to you, I'm disciplining you for your own good, to show you right from wrong. And now, when you've placed your hands on the coffee table as instructed, I'm going to spank you again because you stole money from your father.'

'Wha... what are you talking about now?' she gasped incredulously.

'That's shocked you, hasn't it?'

'I stole money from my father?' she echoed. 'That's ridiculous.'

'So where did you get the money to buy your new clothes?' he quizzed.

'I saved it.'

'When I was here last week your father said he'd lost eighty pounds. You took it from his wallet to buy your clothes, didn't you?'

'No, of course I didn't. Please—'

'Don't you think it odd that your father lost eighty pounds and you sneaked off to town and bought some new clothes? Don't bother denying it, because I was in town that day and I saw you leaving the boutique with a carrier bag. You didn't know that, did you? You didn't know your little deception had been witnessed.'

'I've never stolen money in my life!' she said, aghast, a sickening feeling in the pit of her stomach. 'I've never stolen *anything* in my life. I'd never touch my father's wallet, let alone steal money from him.'

'So how are you going to explain your new clothes?' he cruelly pressed. 'Your father lost eighty pounds, and the very same day you went shopping for new clothes. And to add to the suspicion you didn't tell your parents about your little shopping spree. It doesn't look good, does it?'

Her head spinning with confusion, Emily knew he had her where he wanted her. The photographs, the missing money, her new clothes; the evidence against her - albeit it false and manipulated - was building by the day. What did her scheming neighbour want from her? Did he want sex? Or was spanking her bum enough to satisfy his weird fetish? Whatever it was he wanted, she knew she had little or no choice but to comply with his demands.

Suddenly, standing before him, she reckoned a counter tactic was called for, so she took a deep breath to summon her courage, and opened her dressing gown to display her skimpy white bra and panties to his brooding eyes. He was an older man with greying hair, harmless and pathetic. By showing off her underwear and nubile body she would be able to win him over, even twist him around her little finger and get her own way. Yes, that was the way to get round him.

'You can look but not touch,' she whispered, deciding it best to play along with his pathetic games. 'I know you find me sexy...'

'Sexy?' he snorted. 'Emily, this has nothing to do with sex.'

'You want to touch me, don't you?' she sighed huskily, undeterred by his denial; sure she was very close to turning the tables. 'You want to touch me and—'

'I was right,' he cut in. 'You're proving yourself to be a little tart by offering me your body. Not that I needed any proof.'

'I'm not offering you anything,' she said indignantly. 'I was just—'

'You're way off the mark, young lady. This has nothing to do with sex. It's to do with obedience, discipline, correction. And now you've proved what a tart you are I realise I have a lot of work ahead of me. Now take your dressing gown off completely.'

Suddenly recalling a time at school when a girl in her class had some money stolen, Emily bit her lip. She'd been into the classroom during lunch break to get something from her desk, a teacher saw her, the money went missing. Although there was no proof the finger of blame pointed directly at her. Her father lectured her for two hours, again and again asking whether she'd taken the money. Although she was innocent and had never admitted to the crime, he'd always suspected her. And now she was in a similar situation. Although she was innocent, Arthur thought she'd been offering him sex.

And so defeated yet again, her plan having gone terribly wrong, she slipped her gown off her shoulders and allowed it to fall to the floor. She felt her stomach churn as Arthur gazed at her. She was an inexperienced virgin standing in her underwear before her neighbour, but what else could she now do? Was to comply to his methods of rule the way to get what she wanted, the freedom to go out, no curfews, no questioning...? Was this the way to her holiday in Tenerife? By allowing him to spank her she was sure she'd get what she wanted.

As Arthur scrutinised her shapely body, cast his dark eyes over her gentle curves, she felt a shameful rush of excitement course through her veins. No man had ever seen her like this, and to her horror she realised she was deriving some shocking excitement from standing in her bra and panties before a middle-aged man.

'Place your hands on the coffee table,' he ordered, apparently indifferent to having such a gorgeous teenager standing so close, so nearly naked. 'I'm going to thrash you, Emily,' he decreed, standing and - unseen by the girl as she bent at the waist and positioned her palms on the polished surface - removing his leather belt from his trousers. 'I don't want to have to do this, but...'

'You have no choice?' she whispered anxiously.

'I'm pleased you're seeing sense at last. Hopefully the punishment will do you some good. Let's just hope I can correct your wicked ways before it's too late.'

With the first lash of leather cracking loudly across the tight material of her panties Emily rocked forward and yelped. She'd expected the palm of his hand, not a leather strap. But she was prepared to endure the gruelling thrashing if it meant she would be allowed her freedom in return. Once he realised this was a game of give and take, she was sure he'd chill out and she'd be allowed her liberty. The odd thrashing in return for that? It was a price worth paying.

'Not so hard,' she gasped as the leather belt bit into the stretched silk of her panties, reddening the flesh of her tensed buttocks. 'Arthur, please, that hurts...'

'The harder the better, young lady,' he returned, the belt swatting through the air and flailing the quivering globes of her teenage bottom. 'Perhaps this will teach you a lesson. Offering me sex? Good God, girl, I'm your neighbour and old enough to be your father! Have you no shame?'

'No,' she squealed as the belt again bit into her burning buttocks with a deafening crack, 'please, I didn't offer you—'

'The more you deny your wickedness the harder I'll thrash you,' he promised.

Her knuckles whitening as she pressed her fingertips to the tabletop, she squeezed her eyes shut and tried to endure the cruel thrashing without any more protesting. Counting the lashes, her legs trembling from the strain, she wondered how much more she could endure as she reached eight. Nine... ten... eleven...! Trying to stand upright to halt the merciless flailing of her burning buttocks, she realised how stupid she'd been by launching her foolhardy counteroffensive. Arthur now believed she'd been offering him sex when all she'd tried to do was play along with him a little to get her own way. Her plan had backfired badly, and she knew she was to pay a heavy price for her folly.

'Offering me sex?' Arthur hissed. 'Never have I known such a vulgar whore or been so insulted!'

'Please,' Emily cried. 'Please, stop.'

'Stop?' he echoed, momentarily halting the gruelling beating. 'I've not finished with you yet.'

'Please Arthur, I... I can't take it any more.'

'Put your hands behind your back,' he ordered her, dropping the leather belt to the floor.

'Behind my back?'

'You heard me, do as I say.'

As she straightened up stiffly and did as he ordered, he removed his tie and bound her wrists together with it before she realised what he was doing. He was mad, completely insane. Spanking her and then binding her wrists together - was he out of his mind?

Complying with his continuing instructions she turned and faced him, her head hung. Again wondering why he was treating her like this, she realised he might take more photographs of her.

But he sat in the armchair and smiled at her. Scrutinising her trembling body, first gazing at her shapely breasts and the outlines of her nipples pressing through her snug-fitting bra, he then lowered his eyes and focused on the white triangular cotton of her panties. Her face flushed as embarrassment consumed her, and she meekly asked him why he'd tied her wrists, what he wanted from her.

'It's obvious, isn't it?' he returned. 'You defied me, young lady. Despite my grounding you, you went out. And, it seems, you'd planned to go out this evening too. I have to ensure that you don't defy me again, and the only way I can do that is to restrain you.'

'Please, take the tie off,' she begged, her buttocks burning like fire. 'I won't go out this evening, I promise.'

'I know you won't. Not unless you wish to leave the house in your underwear with your hands tied behind your back.'

'Arthur, please—'

'Don't argue with me, Emily,' he snapped angrily.

'I'm not arguing,' she reasoned. 'All I'm asking is that you take the tie off.'

'You still don't understand, do you? I have bound your wrists to ensure that you don't leave this house. Can't you get that into your pretty head?'

'How long do I have to stay here like this?'

'I'm going to get on with some work now. You'll be quite all right here. Why don't you watch a little television?'

'You're not leaving me like this?' she gasped.

'I have no choice, Emily. You deliberately disobey me, you defy me; this is your own doing, my girl. It's no good crying because you can't be trusted and you're now grounded.'

'But I won't be able to eat like this,' she protested.

'Don't worry; I'll call in every now and then to make sure you're all right. Now I really have to get some work done. I'll lock the backdoor as I leave.'

Watching as he grabbed his belt from the floor and left the room, Emily called after him, begging him to release her. But with the backdoor slamming shut and the lock clicking, she wondered how on earth she'd got herself into this terrible situation. She should never have allowed him to spank her, she should never have... but hindsight was useless, she knew. As she again struggled to free her hands she realised she'd not be able to dress; she would have to remain in her brief underwear until *he* decided otherwise.

The house was quiet, the silence broken only by the ticking of the clock on the mantelpiece. Alone and defenceless, Emily missed the sound of her mother preparing the evening meal, of her father listening to the news on the radio. What had happened? What had gone so terribly wrong?

For an hour she paced the lounge carpet, vowing to get even with her neighbour for the way he'd treated her. Day three, she mused. With each day that passed she was sinking deeper and deeper into his trap. First grounded and now a prisoner in her own home - his grip on her was tightening. Determined to thwart him she decided to make a run for it the minute he released her. She could stay at Christine's house until her parents returned.

'Are you all right?' Arthur called. 'Ah, there you are,' he said, smiling and relaxed as he walked into the lounge and furtively eyed Emily's shapely body. 'Everything okay?'

'Will you please untie me?' she asked. 'I have to go to the loo, I want to put some clothes on, and I need to get something to eat.'

'Of course,' he replied affably. 'But before I release you I have to take out a little insurance.'

'Insurance?' she echoed, inquisitively cocking her head to one side. 'What do you mean?'

'I would imagine you've been making plans while I've been working,' he explained, once again a step or two ahead of her. 'No doubt you've decided to do this and that once you're free. Do you know why I took photographs of you?'

'So you could blackmail me,' she spat. 'It's obvious.'

'Blackmail,' he pondered. 'That's an ugly word, Emily. No, I took the photographs as insurance. Their existence will prevent you from doing something stupid, like running to your parents with tales about me when they return. And if I release you, you'll probably try to get away. That's why I've come up with a neat little insurance policy.'

'Which is?'

'Come upstairs and I'll show you.'

Following him through the hall, Emily frowned as he picked up a carrier bag before climbing the stairs. What, she wondered as he opened her bedroom door and ushered her in, was he up to now?

Closing the door behind her, he rubbed his chin as he looked around the room, and then knelt by the radiator. Taking a chain from the carrier bag he ran it around one of the radiator pipes, threading the end through one of the links and pulling it tight, then he knelt before her as she sat on the end of her bed. In her naivety, Emily didn't realise what his plan was until he fed the free end of the chain around her ankle.

'There,' he said with a triumphant smile, slipping a padlock through the chain links and locking it with a metallic click. 'It's long enough, so now you'll be able to go to the loo, take a shower, sleep, dress yourself...'

'You can't chain me up like a dog,' she gasped. 'For God's sake, you need help.'

'Help?' he sniggered. 'No, I don't think so. I'm quite capable of disciplining you without help.'

'Arthur, please,' she pleaded to his better nature - if he had one, 'this has gone too far.'

'*You* went too far, Emily,' he corrected. 'As I said earlier, I didn't want all this. I was hoping you'd be a good girl and I'd have no need to punish you.'

'What if there's a fire?' she suggested quickly, the sudden idea making her decidedly panicky. 'Have you thought about that?'

'I'm only next door, so you have no need to worry.'

'But I won't be able to—'

'Stop creating problems, Emily,' he interjected. 'This is your punishment, remember that.'

Punishment? Punishment for what? Behaving like any normal teenage girl? Lowering her head she couldn't help but gaze down at her breasts, encased snugly in the tight, white cups of her bra. What was Arthur thinking? Was he looking at their creamy, youthful firmness too? Daring to peep up at him she saw he was indeed focused on them. What were his male thoughts? She'd always been so close to him, she reflected. Going round to visit him, helping in the greenhouse... but what were his thoughts now?

'Are you going to release my hands?' she finally asked, her sweet voice nearly catching in her throat.

'Yes, of course,' he replied, sitting on the chair by the window. 'But before I do...'

'Now what?' she sighed.

'I want to talk to you, Emily.'

'I'm not interested.'

'You're a captive audience, wouldn't you agree?' He chuckled condescendingly. 'I had a long chat with your father last week. You remember, when we sat in the dining room for a couple of hours?' Emily nodded. 'He was talking about you, telling me certain things about you.'

'Such as?'

'He's extremely disappointed in you, Emily.'

'Why?'

'He's reached the stage where he doesn't know what to do. He hasn't told your mother because—'

'Hasn't told her what?'

Arthur lowered his head as if saddened by something, and Emily wondered if he was dreaming up another of his lies. What hadn't her father told her mother? Again wondering whether her trip to Tenerife was worth enduring imprisonment for she gazed at her ankle, the chain running across the floor to the radiator. How far would she allow her neighbour to go in return for a glowing report? Would she do anything he demanded of her?

'As you know, your father is a religious man,' Arthur went on. 'He has morals,

28

beliefs, ideals. We were chatting and he opened his heart to me.'

'What about?' she asked.

'About you, Emily. You see, he knows that you... he told me that you masturbate.'

'*What?*' she gasped, her brown eyes staring at him in disbelief. 'That's absolute rubbish. Never have I heard such—'

'I'm sure your father wasn't making it up when he told me he'd not only heard you masturbating, but seen you.'

'Seen me?' she gasped. 'That's... that's ridiculous. I have never—'

'Yes, so you said,' he cut across her plaintive denial. 'There's obviously no need for me to tell you your father's views on masturbation.'

'I don't believe a word of this,' she whispered incredulously. 'Firstly, I have never masturbated, and secondly, I would have made sure my father wasn't around had I wanted to. You're lying again. All you do is lie.'

'Emily, he *saw* you masturbating,' the man maintained.

'Where?' she challenged. 'When?'

'I don't want to go into the sordid details,' he hedged. 'Suffice to say that your father is gravely disappointed in you.'

'You don't want to go into the details because there are none,' she asserted. 'As I said, you're lying again.'

He let out a chuckle as he gazed at the delightful cups of her bra, the soft flesh they neatly and teasingly contained, and focused on the shadowy valley of her cleavage.

Yet again she had to wonder what he was thinking. What was he planning? Emily was sure her father would never talk about such intimate issues, not even to his trusted friend and neighbour. Such words as *masturbation* would never pass his lips, and certainly not in connection with his daughter. Besides, how would her father have witnessed such an act? He didn't know what went on behind her closed bedroom door.

'All right,' Arthur finally conceded, 'I'll tell you exactly where and when you were masturbating. You were in your bed, and it was last Wednesday evening at just past eleven o'clock.'

'I... I don't know what you're talking about,' Emily stammered defensively.

'Your father got out of bed to go to the bathroom. As he passed your bedroom door he thought he heard you whispering something. He was concerned and listened for a while, wondering if you were unwell. And not wanting to invade your privacy he eventually checked you were okay by kneeling down and peering through the keyhole.' Arthur paused, watching the lovely girl as he let the enormity of his words sink in to her pretty head. 'There's no need for me to describe to you the sight that met his eyes, is there?' he added.

Her face flushing, Emily now knew Arthur wasn't lying. That Wednesday night she had massaged her clitoris until she orgasmed.

'Guilty,' Arthur announced sternly, his dark eyes staring accusingly at her.

Guilty? Yes, she was guilty of masturbating, and dismayed to think he had seen her she wondered how she could ever face him again. Loath to imagine what he thought of her, she recalled stifling her gasps of pleasure as her climax rocked her naked body.

'There's no point in lying about it, Emily,' Arthur said. 'You masturbate, don't you?'

'Is that what this is all about?' she asked him.

'It really doesn't have a great deal to do with your being home by ten or having Christine sleep over. As you can imagine, your father was shocked by what he witnessed. He was visibly choked, Emily.'

'He was mistaken,' she proffered weakly. 'I... I had a stomach ache and... and...'

'He wasn't mistaken.'

'So what has this to do with the way you've treated me?' she said futilely. 'In fact, what has it got to do with you at all?'

'Your father and I have been good friends for many years. He not only trusts me, but he knows he can confide in me. And having seen what he did the reason he wants me to keep such a close eye on you is obvious, surely, even to you. He's afraid you'll go off the rails completely without them here.'

'But why have you beaten me?' she asked. 'Why have you chained me up like a dog?'

'Because you need to learn, young lady,' he said simply. 'Your father now believes he's failed miserably in bringing you up to be a respectable young lady. You've hurt him deeply, and as he's a very good friend of mine, I can't stand by and watch you continue to hurt him.'

'All I did was...' she whispered. 'I mean, all I did was...'

'Your father is at a loss what to do with you. You might believe masturbation is harmless enough, but that's not the way he sees it. I've called you a slut and a tart, and I didn't want to have to tell you this but, well, they were his words, Emily, not mine.'

'My... my father called me that?' Tears sparkled in her eyes and threatened to cascade down her rosy cheeks.

'Yes, he did,' Arthur confirmed, nodding gravely. 'Don't get me wrong; he still loves you very much. It's just that you've disappointed him hugely. What you did went against everything your father believes in, everything he stands for. Can't you see that?'

'Yes, yes I can,' she admitted, sniffing softly. 'But what I can't see is why you've spanked me, thrashed me with a leather belt and treated me no better than an animal.'

'As I said, I'm not prepared to stand by and watch you hurt your father,' he said piously. 'As soon as he'd left the house you dressed up like a tart and went out drinking. The following night you rolled in at gone two o'clock, having been drinking again, and I'm not prepared to watch you turn into a brazen whore and destroy your parents.'

'All right, I've seen the error of my ways,' she sobbed. 'Let's start again, Arthur, please. *Please* take this chain off me.'

'I can't do that, Emily. I can't do that because, like your father, I can't trust you. I'll release your hands but the chain stays put. I'll be back later to make you something to eat, and in the meantime I suggest you do some serious thinking.'

As he undid and removed his tie and left the room, Emily hung her head and cried. Again dreading to think how she was ever going to face her father, she wondered how many times he'd heard or seen her masturbating. She only did it to find some solace, she reflected, to bring a little excitement and pleasure into her mundane life. Shame and embarrassment engulfing her, she went to the window and gazed down at the back garden, the chain following her.

'A caged bird,' she murmured, watching a sparrow fluttering from branch to branch in the apple tree. But her misdemeanours had nothing to do with her next-door neighbour, she again thought. He had no right to punish her, whatever he said to justify it. This was between her and her parents. It had nothing to do with Arthur. Why was he so involved?

Chapter 4

Going into her parents' bedroom, the chain dragging behind her across the landing, Emily sat on their bed and lifted the bedside phone. Restricted, imprisoned, she'd been chained like an animal for over an hour. She had to escape this nightmare. Christine would help, she knew, as she tapped the buttons and listened to the ringing tone. Whatever happened, whatever the outcome, she was determined to escape her neighbour's loathsome clutches.

'Hi, it's me,' she said softly as Christine answered.

'Hi, Emily. You sound down. Are you all right?'

'No, not really.'

'What's the problem?'

'Everything. I - I can't leave the house.'

'Why ever not?'

'Can you come round?'

'Yes, yes of course.'

'Only, don't let Arthur see you. Come in through the back gate and keep behind the bushes until you reach the backdoor.'

'What is this all about, Emily?' Her friend was sounding increasingly worried.

'I'll explain when you get here, although I don't know how you're going to get into the house.'

'Emily, what is going on?

'Just get here as soon as you can.'

'All right, I'm on my way.'

Replacing the receiver and returning to her bedroom, Emily tugged a T-shirt over her head and gazed out of the window again. The sun shining, the birds singing, the sound of a lawnmower in the distance - she was surrounded by the sights and sounds of freedom, and yet...

Again looking down at her chain of bondage, she again wondered how Christine was going to get into the house. There was no point in dropping the front door key out of the window because the latch was up. And the chain was too short to allow her to go downstairs and open the door.

With pictures of her father spying through the keyhole of her bedroom door looming in her tormented mind, she again hung her head as a tear rolled down her cheek. What must he have thought? Had he watched as she reached her climax? Had he watched as she arched her back and quivered uncontrollably in the grip of her orgasm...?

Half an hour later she saw Christine in the alleyway, and watched the girl slip through the back gate and make her way slowly up the garden path.

Emily held her hand to her mouth as she watched through the net curtains. If Arthur saw her friend, if he discovered that Emily had phoned her... the consequences didn't bear thinking about. But with no way into the house there was nothing Christine could do anyway. It had been a mistake to phone her, Emily realised, and then froze as Arthur also appeared through the back gate.

'Hello, Christine,' he said, making the girl jump.

'Oh, erm... hi,' Christine replied, spinning round, clearly flustered.

'What are you doing here?' he asked.

'I, um... I've come to see Emily,' she stammered.

'She's gone out,' he told her. 'I saw her leave about ten minutes ago.'

'Gone out?' Christine echoed, her expression depicting confusion.

'No,' Emily gasped, her stomach sinking as she could just make out their muffled conversation. She couldn't believe this.

'Do you know where she's gone?' Christine asked, frowning at Arthur.

'No, I don't. I saw her from my office window about ten minutes ago.'

'Oh, right. Well, I'll probably talk to her later, then.'

Watching Christine leave the garden, Emily knew she should have guessed that Arthur would be lurking. How was he able to watch the house all the time? Unless he had cameras...

Her eyes widening in alarm as he walked up the path towards the backdoor, she decided to say nothing about Christine. If he questioned her she'd deny phoning her friend, deny having spoken to her. Hearing the backdoor open she sat on her bed and gazed out to the landing.

'Everything all right?' Arthur asked, entering her bedroom a few moments later and standing before her.

'Oh, everything's fine,' she returned sarcastically. 'I'm chained up like a dog, I can't dress because of the chain, I can't even feed myself.'

'I've decided to allow you out this evening,' he announced, sitting beside her on the bed. 'As long as you're home by ten, you can go out.'

'Oh, er, right,' she said, caught somewhat by surprise, wondering why he'd changed his tune. Was this another trick?

As he flickered his eyes to the outline of her nipples pressing through her white bra, she wondered what he'd want in return for allowing her out. He was becoming less guarded in the way he looked at her, but he'd not made any sexual overtures toward her. Did he want sex with her? Or perhaps he really did just get his kicks from spanking her. Was that his fantasy, his turn on? His eyes lowering to her panties, focusing on the cotton 'V' disappearing between her smooth thighs, cosseting her soft pubic curls, he licked his lips.

'I'm a fair man, Emily,' he said, his gaze still locked to her thighs and her skimpy panties. 'You misbehaved, and you've been punished. So now you may go out, as long as you're home by ten.'

'Thanks,' she murmured, smiling at him warily.

'Would you like a cup of tea now?' he asked, out of the blue, his eyes lifting to hers.

'Um, yes, yes please,' she said gratefully.

'I'll go home and make it,' he said. 'With all due respect, I've never liked the tea your parents buy. I won't be a minute.'

Her mind flooding with thoughts of Jack as Arthur left the house, she felt her stomach lurch. She was going to meet him after all, she mused happily. Of course she'd have to be home by ten if she was to avoid more trouble, but that wouldn't present too much of a problem. She'd tell Jack she had relations visiting and had to get back to see them.

Perhaps Arthur wasn't so bad after all, she reflected. He'd said he was trying to make a better person of her and only had her best interests at heart. But he'd spanked and belted her poor bottom, bound her wrists and chained her to the radiator. No, he was bad and she had to get away, she decided. She'd go out for the evening and not come home. She'd stay with Christine until her parents got back from holiday, that's what she'd do.

Dashing into her parents' bedroom as the phone rang, she hoped creepy Arthur would be a few minutes longer as she lifted the receiver.

'I'm on my mobile,' Christine gabbled. 'Where did you get to? Why did you ask me to come round and then go out?'

'I didn't go out,' Emily replied. 'I'm in my room. I saw you through my window, talking to Arthur.'

'He said you'd gone out. What's going on, Emily? What's this all about?'

'Christine, I'm chained to my bedroom radiator,' Emily told her friend. 'Arthur bound my wrists together with a tie and—'

'He did what?' Christine squealed.

'I'm only in my underwear and there's a chain from my ankle to the radiator,' Emily elaborated.

'You've been watching too much television,' the girl giggled. 'The old man from next door chained you to the radiator? You haven't been sitting in the sun for too long, have you?'

'Of course not,' Emily denied desperately. 'Look, I have to go. Arthur will be back in a minute.'

Her friend chuckled again in her ear. 'I think you need some help, Ems.'

'Too right I do,' the chained girl agreed, 'and I've just had an idea. Where are you?'

'Just down the road.'

'Okay, come round now. He's gone back to his house to get me a cup of tea. The backdoor might be unlocked, so once he's up in my room slip into the house and hide in the dining room until he's gone.'

'Ems, I really don't think—'

'Just do it, Chrissie, please,' Emily implored.

'All right, anything you say. Although I really don't think you—'

'I'll explain everything later. Just don't let him see or hear you.'

Dashing back to her room and sitting again on the bed, Emily reckoned Arthur was playing games with her. Saying she was allowed out that evening, smiling at her, being nice; what was he up to? What was he after? Sure that he had no intention of releasing her, she planned that Christine would use her father's hacksaw to cut through the chain. And once she was free she'd leave the house, stay at Christine's place until her parents returned, and...

Trying not to plan too far ahead as she heard Arthur trudging up the stairs, she prayed for her plan to work.

'One tea,' Arthur said, placing the mug on the bedside table.

'Thank you, Arthur,' she said sweetly. 'When will you release me?' she asked. 'If I'm going out this evening I need to—'

'There's plenty of time,' he said, again sitting beside her on the bed. 'You have lovely legs, my dear,' he suddenly said, alarming her though she tried not to show it. 'In fact, you have a lovely body, full stop. You're a very attractive girl.'

'Yes, well,' she murmured uncomfortably, shuddering inwardly as his eyes crawled over her form.

'I mean it,' he maintained. 'I've had my eye on you for a while now.'

'Had your eye on me?' She averted her gaze as his eyes drilled into hers. 'What do you mean?'

'I've been watching you grow into an extremely attractive young lady,' he qualified.

'Oh, I see.' Poor Emily didn't know what else to say.

'Yes, I've kept a close watch on you, Emily,' he mused, almost to himself, and as his gaze lowered again and crawled over the triangular patch of cotton concealing her intimacies, Emily knew she had to get away. She didn't know who he was any more, what he'd become. She recalled the many times she'd helped him in his greenhouse, and the time he suggested she take her T-shirt off as the temperature reached the nineties. She didn't, of course, but was it the heat in the greenhouse that had him sweating so much, or the thought of seeing her without her T-shirt on...?

'It's a shame your father saw you masturbating,' he said, breaking into Emily's thoughts. 'That really did upset him.'

'Yes, I know it must have,' she sighed, hoping he didn't want to discuss that again.

'To see his daughter doing such a vulgar thing must have been, well, don't get me wrong; I have nothing against you masturbating. I understand it's only natural in a girl of your age. How often do you masturbate?'

Emily's mouth gaped and she didn't know how to answer that. 'I... I don't,' she stumbled unconvincingly. 'What I mean is, I...'

'It's all right. I quite understand that you find the subject embarrassing. In future, I suggest you wait until your parents are out before indulging yourself in such a way.'

'Yes,' she breathed, wondering what else she could say and where this was leading.

'Right, I have a couple of phone calls to make before I can—'

'I thought you were going to release me?'

'I'll only be ten minutes, and then I'll come back and release you so you can get ready to go out this evening.'

Hoping Christine was hiding in the dining room, Emily sipped her tea as she listened to Arthur going downstairs. Freedom was close, she was sure as she heard the backdoor close. Once the chain had been cut she'd slip out of the front and make her escape. Though what she'd tell her parents she had no idea. Christine had obviously thought her mad when she told her about the chain and things. There was no way her parents would believe such an outrageous story.

Hearing a noise downstairs Emily's spirits rose. Calling out for her friend to come up to her room, she sat upright and waited expectantly for her to appear. There was a hacksaw in the toolbox in the under-stairs cupboard. Christine would have no trouble cutting through the chain. Perhaps she could even cut off the padlock. Then once dressed, Emily would flee from her house and Arthur. He'd have a fit when he discovered his prisoner gone, she mused, again calling out for Christine, but that was his problem.

'Are you expecting your friend?' Arthur asked, his expression one of inert friendliness as he leaned against the doorway, at odds with the length of rope he twisted ominously around his fists.

'I, um, I thought I heard her calling through the letterbox,' Emily hastily lied, her cheeks flushing, her hands trembling as she focused on the rope with wide, anxious eyes.

'Really?' he said genially. 'And how would she have been able to get into the house? You called out and told her to come up to your bedroom, but she doesn't have a key, does she?'

'No, I...' Emily's mind scrambled around for something remotely believable to say. 'I thought... um, I thought...'

'You thought she'd slip in through the backdoor and wait until I'd gone,' he said for her, watching her discomfort. 'Is that it?'

'No, of course not,' she blustered fearfully.

'I believe you spoke to her on the phone, Emily. I believe you told her you're chained to the radiator in your bedroom.'

'No, I didn't, please,' she desperately denied, shaking her head, her eyes watching his every little move.

'Are you going to persist with your lies? You spoke to her on the phone and told her to come here to help you.'

'I said nothing of the sort,' Emily returned, wondering how he knew.

'Had I not locked the backdoor when I came up with your tea, your plan might have worked,' he said pensively.

'There *was* no plan,' she said shakily, her eyes transfixed by the rope dangling threateningly from his hands.

'Oh dear,' he sighed, shaking his head theatrically, 'what a great shame. I thought I could trust you, but clearly I can't.'

'Arthur, I haven't done anything,' she repeated worriedly.

'Yes, you have, you've put paid to your going out this evening.'

'Arthur, please, I didn't say anything to Christine. I haven't seen her or spoken to her today.'

'Lies tumble from your lips with such ease it's frightening,' he derided. 'Probably because of years of lying to your parents.'

'I have never lied to my parents,' she protested.

'All I can think is that you must enjoy being punished,' he added, as though deaf to her objection.

'Arthur, please don't do this any more,' she beseeched plaintively, wondering when this unjust torment would end.

'Why have you done this, Emily? I was going to allow you out this evening. I thought that, well, it doesn't matter what I thought. What does matter is your persistent poor behaviour.'

Twisting the rope around his hands as he stood beside the bed, his dark eyes devoid of emotion, he gazed down at Emily's breasts, and then her shapely thighs. Crossing her legs self-consciously she focused on the rope, wondering whether she should make a stand against the brute. There was more than enough evidence against her - contrived or not - to put paid to her holiday in Tenerife, and to allow Arthur to punish her again wouldn't change that. She'd not now be going on holiday later in the summer, or to the wine bar that evening to meet Jack, so she had nothing to lose now, she knew.

'But I'll give you the benefit of the doubt this time,' Arthur said, much to her amazement. 'I suppose it is possible you thought you heard Christine calling through the letterbox.'

'I did,' Emily said excitedly. 'Really, I did.'

'All right, all right,' he chuckled benevolently, 'you can go out this evening. But you'll take three lashes of the rope first to remind you not to misbehave again.'

Emily's cruelly raised spirits sank instantly and her hopeful smile vanished. 'No, please.'

'The choice is yours,' he went on regardless. 'Three lashes and then you'll be allowed out. What's it to be?'

'Only three?' she asked, tentatively weighing up her options.

'Three will be enough to give you a taste of what you'll get if you're late home again,' he confirmed. 'So if you're in agreement, turn round and lie on your front.'

Reluctantly adopting the required position, Emily squeezed her eyes shut and tensed her buttocks in readiness for the first bite of the rope. This was to be the last time, she vowed to herself. Three lashes not only in return for a night out, but her ultimate escape too. She'd ring Chrissie and arrange to stay at her house, and even if Arthur discovered where she was there'd be nothing he could do to get his hands on her again. Three lashes, and then she'd be free of the creep.

'No...' she cried into her quilt as the rope slashed through the air and landed across the cotton-covered globes of her clenched bottom with a sickening crack.

'Number one,' Arthur counted, raising the rope above his head again.

With her young body trembling uncontrollably, Emily held her breath and waited for the second gruelling bite. Arthur was making her wait, she knew, sadistically enjoying every second of her torture. This was how he got his kicks. Inhaling deeply and anxiously holding her breath, she buried her face in her pillow as she waited in trepidation for the second strike.

'*Please*...!' Her distraught wail was muffled as the rope flailed her tensed bottom, the force of the blow making it quiver with vitality inside her tight, white panties.

'Number two,' Arthur pronounced, again raising the rope above his head. 'One more, Emily. Just one more, and then you may go out for the evening.'

'Yes, yes,' she whimpered, tears soaking into the pillow as she held her breath and clenched her burning buttocks.

With the crack of the last and final strike echoing around her bedroom, she let out another pitiful wail. She'd done it, she thought. She'd endured the evil monster's punishment and would now not only be free to leave the house, but free of him for good. Clutching her scalded rear, she slowly managed to sit upright. Freedom was so close. She could almost smell the refreshing air of the outside world. Wiping the tears from her flushed cheeks, her head hung low, she prayed for the man to keep his side of the bargain and release her from her living hell.

'I didn't want to have to do that,' he said, dropping the rope on the end of the bed. 'However, now you've taken your punishment you may go out this evening.'

'Please, take the chain off,' she whimpered, again wiping the tears from her eyes with the back of her hand. 'Just let me get out of here for a while.'

'All in good time, Emily,' he said, brushing her tousled hair away from her flushed brow. 'All in good time.'

'What is it now?' she asked. 'Is this another trick?'

'A trick?' he echoed indignantly. 'Of course it's not a trick. I'm a man of my word, young lady. You should know that. But I've left the padlock key at my place, so I'll have to go and get it. I'll only be a couple of minutes. Oh, by the way, how are you for money?'

'Money?' she said, perplexed by his question. 'Well, I'm...'

'I'll give you twenty pounds. That should be enough for you to have a nice evening out.'

'Erm, right, thanks,' she said, somewhat bemused by the gesture, unsure of his motives. Why was he giving her money? He was baiting her, she was sure. It must have occurred to him that she'd make a run for it once free. He was taunting her, giving her hope only to plunge her into the depths of despair again with his evil games.

After half an hour of awaiting his return with the key, she knew she was right. She wasn't to be given her freedom at all. Desperate now, her buttocks throbbing, she wondered whether to ring Christine again and ask her to bring her father round. He would sort creepy Arthur out. She couldn't sit on her bed chained to the radiator all night. She was going to have to do something.

Suddenly the front doorbell rang and she wondered whether her best friend had come back to help. Then hearing the backdoor open and close she sat upright, tense and alert, watching the top of the stairs through the open bedroom door. Had Arthur brought the key? Was she about to be released from the loathsome chain? The front doorbell rang again and she frowned, puzzled. Was this another of his tricks, or had one of their other neighbours called round to see her? Then she heard the front door opening and strained her ears to hear what Arthur was saying.

'She's gone out,' he said, he lied.

'Oh, right,' a male responded. 'I just thought... but if she's gone out... it doesn't matter.'

'Do you want me to tell her you called?' Arthur asked politely.

'No, that's okay... I'm meeting her tonight anyway... at the wine bar.'

'Really? What time?'

'Eight... her friend gave me her address.'

'She's probably gone there to meet you already,' Arthur suggested. 'What did you say your name was?'

'Jack... you must be her father.'

'No, no,' Arthur said, 'I'm just a friend of the family. Look, if she comes back I'll tell her you called.'

'Thanks,' called Jack's fading voice as he retreated up the garden path.

Fuming, Emily clenched her fists as she heard the front door close. She should have called out for Jack to help her, but she just didn't react to the surprise of hearing his voice quickly enough.

'So, you'd planned to meet a youth at a wine bar,' Arthur stated as he appeared at the top of the stairs and walked into her bedroom.

'What of it?' Emily challenged. 'As I've repeatedly told you, I'm eighteen and I can do what I want.'

She tensed, regretting her impulsive response whilst awaiting a resurgence of the weirdo's wrath, but Arthur suddenly smiled broadly and moved right in front of her, looking down into her eyes.

'You're right, Emily,' he said, taking a small key from his trouser pocket and stooping to release her ankle. 'There, now you're free to go out, just as I promised. If you hurry you should be in time to meet Jack.'

38

Frowning cautiously, Emily stood up. Was this another trick? What was his game? Perhaps he'd decided he'd gone too far, she mused, grabbing her miniskirt from her wardrobe and pulling it up her legs. Then slipping her shoes on she took her blouse from the wardrobe, oblivious to the watching man so relieved was she that this was her chance to escape.

He focused on the fullness of her bra, snugly holding her creamy breasts, and the smooth plain of her stomach as she slipped her arms into the blouse's short sleeves. He sat on the chair by the window and eyed her naked legs. 'Have a good time,' he called as she finished buttoning her blouse and skipped down the stairs.

'Yes, I will,' she called back up, reaching the front door as he appeared at the top of the stairs.

'Oh, just before you go,' he said.

'Yes?' Emily stood holding the door open, looking up at him. With the warm evening breeze wafting around her naked legs she was almost free. 'What is it?'

'Here's the twenty pounds I promised you,' he said, holding out a crisp note as he descended the stairs and stood before her in the hall.

'No, thanks, you don't have to,' she said.

'I thought you wanted to meet Jack at the wine bar,' he said, looking put out.

'I do, but you don't have to...' she paused, scrutinising the man closely with her wide, innocent eyes. 'What is it you want? Tell me, Arthur. What do you want from me?'

'Nothing more than respect, good behaviour and obedience, Emily,' he said simply.

'And you're prepared to threaten and blackmail me so I behave as you want me to?'

'Can we move away from such words as threat and blackmail?' he said, his expression one of distaste. 'They're ugly words and they have no place here.'

'They have *every* place here,' she argued. 'They couldn't be more fitting words for the way you're treating me.'

'Here,' he said, looking uncomfortable with the subject and changing it by offering her the money again, 'why don't you go out and enjoy yourself? I'll see you when you get home, at ten o'clock. You will be home by ten, won't you?'

'What choice do I have?' she said, taking the money and putting it in her small shoulder bag.

'Good. That's settled then. And we'll have a cosy little chat when you get home.'

Leaving the house Emily walked briskly down the street, but gradually her pace faltered and she slowed to a halt. She couldn't meet Jack at the wine bar, she knew, or run away from home as she'd planned to. How could she when she was so worried about Arthur, the accusation of the missing money, the report book, the photographs, and what he might do with them if she provoked him?

Riddled with confusion, doubts and anxieties, she made her way to the park, the evening sun warming her face and legs, and wondered what Arthur might do when she got home. Would he find an excuse to punish her again?

Sitting on a bench she looked out across the park. There was a man walking a dog, a young woman pushing a pram, kids playing on the swings. They were free to live their lives, whereas Arthur had so much on her now that she daren't cross him. But why, she wondered for the umpteenth time, was he doing all this? What *did* he want from her?

Trying to relax she watched the orange sun sinking behind the trees. Christine would be in the wine bar, and Jack would be wondering why Emily had stood him up. Perhaps they'd get together - Jack buying the drinks, Christine chatting him up. They were probably having a great time, but what did Emily's evening hold - another unjust punishment? With her buttocks still pulsing slightly from her latest beating, she knew she dare not be a minute late getting back home - or she'd pay for it.

Chapter 5

Emily slipped the key into the lock, wondering fearfully if Arthur was inside waiting for her as the door opened. Was he in the lounge, waiting, lurking? It didn't feel like home any more. It was just a house, a place to live. With despondency and disquiet setting in Emily closed the door and hovered uncertainly in the hall. Arthur wouldn't miss an opportunity to chastise her, would he? Checking her watch as she crept into the lounge, she sighed with relief. It was nine forty-five. She wasn't late, and Arthur wasn't there. He had no excuse to punish her again. But where was he? *Why* wasn't he waiting for her?

Wondering whether he was lurking in her bedroom, she climbed the stairs cautiously. Arthur was a control freak and he'd go to any lengths to control her. But breathing another sigh of relief as she looked around her room, she couldn't understand why he wasn't in the house. Perhaps he'd gone out for the night, she thought, deciding to go back down and slip the catch on the front door and jam a chair against the backdoor.

She couldn't live like this; worrying, constantly fearful, riddled with anxieties. She had to try to forget about Arthur, to calm her mind and relax. With the house secure she'd at least get a good night's sleep, and she felt a little easier as she filled the kettle for a nice, hot, comforting herbal tea.

'Well done,' Arthur said, suddenly looming in the kitchen doorway.

'Shit!' Emily shrieked, almost dropping the kettle and holding her throat as her heart raced. 'You frightened the living daylights out of me!'

'You're a quarter of an hour early,' he carried on calmly. 'That's good, Emily. You see, you can do it when you try.'

'How did you get in?' she asked, feeling faint and having to put the kettle on the worktop before she did drop it.

'With my front door key, of course,' he answered simply. 'I've been waiting for you in the dining room.'

'Skulking in the dining room more like,' she snapped, her pulse still racing. 'What do you want now, at this time?'

'As I said earlier, I thought we'd have a cosy little chat.'

'But I'm tired, Arthur,' Emily complained. 'I want to go to bed, so do you mind leaving instead? We can have a chat tomorrow, if you like.'

'I see you've got the kettle on,' he said, ignoring her request. 'I'll have a drink with you before I go.'

Making two mugs of steaming peppermint tea, Emily feared there was no escaping the man.

'Did you meet Jack?' he asked, accepting the hot drink she passed to him and then leading the way into the lounge as though he knew she'd follow without having to be told to.

'No, no I didn't,' she replied, following his back.

'Oh, that's a shame,' he said, with a distinct lack of sincerity.

'I didn't go to the bar,' she divulged. 'Not that it has anything to do with you.'

'Oh, Emily,' he said, placing his mug on the mantelpiece, 'the way you talk to me with such little respect really disappoints me. I've been good to you - very good.'

'Good to me?' she scoffed, laughing at the irony of his remark. 'How on earth do you work that out?'

'This is the third consecutive night you've been out,' he reasoned, as if that constituted being very good to her.

'What is it you want from me, Arthur?' she asked wearily. 'Why are you always coming round here, dreaming up excuses to punish me? Please just tell me; what do you want?'

'To make a better person of you,' he said. 'Discipline and obedience—'

'Oh please, don't start that nonsense again,' she said impatiently. 'To make a better person of me? By tying my wrists and chaining me to a radiator, spanking me and thrashing me with a leather belt? You said you wanted to have a chat, so let's talk about this. You've made my life hell since my parents went away. I would have been perfectly all right on my own, but because of you, because of all this trouble you've caused—'

'Now just a minute,' he snapped, sitting on the sofa and fleetingly eyeing her thighs. '*You* caused all this trouble, Emily. I've done nothing except try and do what's best for you.'

'You're mad,' she said. 'Totally nuts. You've done all this, not me.'

'Did I tell you to go out dressed like a tart?' he asked. 'Did I?'

'No, but...'

'Did I tell you to go out and get tipsy and then come home late?'

'No, you didn't.' Already she was floundering again.

'No, of course I didn't. It had nothing to do with me, Emily. Your mother said she wanted you home by ten, and I dutifully reminded you of that only an hour before you went out. To blame me for your behaviour is an insult to my intelligence and disrespectful in the extreme.'

'I wasn't blaming you for my behaviour.'

'Weren't you? You mentioned *all this trouble* I've caused. You said you would have been perfectly all right on your own.'

'I would have been fine on my own.'

'Yes, I'm sure you would. Out all night, drinking and misbehaving. It seems you're blaming me for the trouble you've landed yourself in, when all I've tried to do is keep you out of trouble.'

'You know very well what I meant,' she persisted doggedly.

'No, I don't. I have done everything I can to keep you out of trouble. Last night, for example, even though I'd told you not to go out you disobeyed and came rolling in at two in the morning. Your mother specifically said that she wanted you home by ten. Eleven-thirty the first night, and two o'clock the second.'

As he rambled on, lecturing her, Emily knew it was hopeless. She'd worn her sexy new blouse and miniskirt, gone out drinking and arrived home late - twice. She couldn't deny it, and he knew that.

And then there was the matter of her father's missing money, and the photographs. Things weren't looking at all good. But still none of this had anything to do with her next-door neighbour. She would have been perfectly all right on her own. She'd have enjoyed a drink with Christine and got home late, but her parents would have been none the wiser. It was only Arthur's intervention, his interference and threats, that were causing the problems.

'Get out, Arthur,' Emily said. 'I've just about had enough of you and your so called discipline.'

The man stared at her for some moments, as though trying to come to terms with the audacity of her outburst. 'I think I'd better phone your father,' he stated dourly.

'He's in Spain,' she said, somewhat cheekily but too tired to care. 'How are you going to phone him?'

'He gave me the number of the hotel before he left,' Arthur disclosed. 'Just in case of an emergency, you understand. And in my opinion this is an emergency. Because of your questionable behaviour your parents will have to cut short their holiday and come home.'

Sinking into the armchair Emily couldn't believe he'd do such a thing - to ruin her parents' holiday, to drag them home when there was nothing wrong. But he *would* do it, she knew as he gazed blatantly at her thighs, and looking down she realised he was able to glimpse the white 'V' of her panties tight between them. Her short skirt had ridden up slightly, so she blushed and crossed her legs, feeling extremely uncomfortable under his unsettling scrutiny. This had gone too far, she decided. She was going to have to make a stand, and knew she had to discover exactly what it was he wanted from her.

'Well?' he demanded, lifting his eyes to hers, and then lowering them again, this time to her deep cleavage, exposed by the open neck of her blouse. 'Shall I ring your father?'

'If you do that you'll put an end to your games,' she said, with a note of triumph.

'Games?' he echoed.

'If you ring my parents and they come home, your games will have to end.'

'I'm not playing games, Emily,' he snorted. 'You might think this a game but, as far as I'm concerned, this is deadly serious. What about your holiday in Tenerife? If I ring your father and tell him what you've been up to, if he's forced to come home because of your behaviour, well, need I say more?'

'I've changed my mind about Tenerife,' she lied. 'I was looking forward to it, but now I'm really not that bothered.'

'You *think* I'm bluffing about ringing your father, but I *know* you're bluffing about Tenerife. So I'll call your bluff, young lady; I'll go and ring your father now.'

Watching him take a piece of paper from his jacket pocket, Emily didn't know what to do as he went into the hall and picked up the phone. She followed him and watched as he tapped the numbers, imagining her parents arriving home early and going mad at her. She'd be grounded for months and they'd disown her. Glancing at the piece of paper, her mind racing, she saw it was a foreign number. But was it the hotel in Spain? What if he wasn't bluffing? As he spoke into the receiver and asked someone whether it was possible to speak to her father, she quickly stooped and tugged the cable from the wall socket.

'All right,' she conceded, 'you win.'

'No one wins, Emily,' he said, replacing the receiver and returning to the lounge. 'As I said, this isn't a game. There are no winners or losers. Apart from your parents, that is.' Sitting on the sofa he looked up at her as she stood before him. 'And now that you realise this isn't a game, perhaps you'll change your attitude.'

'What is it you want from me, Arthur?' she asked resignedly. 'Come on, tell me what this is really about.'

He seemed hesitant as he gazed into the brown pools of her questioning eyes. Then slowly looking her shapely form over from head to toe, he rubbed his chin pensively. Emily wondered what he was thinking, what he was planning. Why wouldn't he be honest with her? Why not tell her exactly what he was after? Was he embarrassed? Did he want sex with her, but couldn't find the words to admit it, to himself or to her?

'Well?' she quietly urged. 'Please tell me.'

'Before we go any further,' he began, his eyes fixed on her legs, 'you'll call me Mr Price.'

'Mr Price?' she queried. 'Why should I do that?'

'From now on you will call me Mr Price,' he reiterated, brushing aside her question. 'Unless you want me to ring your parents, that is.'

'But...'

'Do you understand?'

Emily hesitated, and then sighed. 'Yes,' she said, having no choice other than to play along with him.

'Yes, what?' he pressed.

'Yes, Mr Price,' she whispered.

He nodded, with a hint of satisfaction glinting in his eyes. 'That's more like it,' he drawled. 'Your behaviour thus far has been appalling, hasn't it?'

'No—'

'Hasn't it, Emily?'

Her cheeks coloured and she lowered her gaze to the carpet. 'Yes,' she said meekly. 'Yes, Mr Price.'

'Go and get the rope from your bedroom,' he ordered.

'The rope? What are you going to do?'

'Just get the rope, young lady.'

Climbing the stairs, Emily again wondered how she'd got herself into this mess. Although she had another brief chance to escape, there was little point; Arthur would simply ring her father and tell him she'd gone missing. They'd cut short their holiday and come home, so even without her chain, she realised, she was trapped in the house - a prisoner in her own home.

She was in for a severe thrashing, she guessed, and there was no way out of it. And even though that was bad enough, whatever sort of man he was he at least wouldn't coerce her into having sex with him - would he?

'Good girl,' he said as she returned to the lounge with the rope dangling from one trembling hand. 'Now, pull the armchair round and, well, you know what to do.'

'Why are you going to punish me again?' she asked, dragging the chair into the centre of the room. 'What am I supposed to have done this time?'

'Your little show of defiance, Emily,' he explained reasonably, as though it was a perfectly understandable reason for beating her. 'I will not tolerate such insubordination. Oh, and remember to call me Mr Price.'

Bending over the back of the chair, Emily closed her eyes and resigned herself to the fact that she was completely under the creep's control. There was no point in arguing with him or trying to discuss the situation. To protest would not only be futile, but also land her in dire trouble with her parents. She couldn't fight and she couldn't run. Arthur had won, she reflected miserably as he knelt behind her on one knee and tied each of her ankles to the chair legs. This wasn't a game, but Arthur had won it nonetheless.

With her feet wide apart and her bottom positioned vulnerably, she said nothing as he folded her skirt up over her waist and ran his knuckles against the smooth cotton of her white panties. What, she wondered, was it to be this time - a spanking with the palm of his hand or a spiteful beating with the leather belt? But then he left the room and she heard the backdoor open and close, and she frowned. What was he up to now?

Wondering whether to untie the ropes she straightened up, her skirt falling to veil her tight panties. She'd have no problem sitting on the floor and removing the bonds, but if Arthur came back she'd be in even bigger trouble. No, it was best to wait obediently for a while, she decided, and then heard the backdoor open and close again and was glad she'd not done anything rash.

'Sorry to have kept you waiting,' he said as he appeared, flexing a bamboo cane. 'I couldn't decide which implement to use.'

'No,' she gasped, staring wide-eyed in horror at the threatening stick. 'Mr Price, please—'

'Spanking wouldn't be punishment enough,' he cut in, 'and my belt doesn't really fit the crime, either.'

'Crime?' she squealed. 'For God's sake, Arthur, what crime?'

'For your continuing disrespectful behaviour, Emily, and for not calling me Mr Price,' he pronounced. 'Only the cane will do.'

'Please, you can't—'

'I had decided on four lashes,' he continued, 'but as you're determined to resist my authority—'

'I'm not, Mr Price,' she pleaded, 'honestly I'm not.'

'Your continual insubordination leaves me no other choice.' The man was resolute, and Emily knew it was hopeless to defy him.

'All right...' she whispered despondently, 'Mr Price.'

'Gratifying though it is,' he said coldly, pressing against her shoulder and easing her back over the chair, then folding her skirt up again, 'your compliance is rather late. That's what this discipline is all about, Emily; learning to behave well, thus avoiding punishment. This is all your own doing, my girl.' He paused as he gazed at the delicate material of her panties stretching faithfully to the rounded cheeks of her teenage bottom. 'This is your own doing, but I'm a fair man, so I won't use the cane... not this time.'

As he rolled her panties down to her thighs, exposing her clenched buttocks, she let out a rush of breath. He was gazing at her naked bottom, she knew. His beady eyes would be focusing on the smooth cheeks, eyeing the tightly closed valley between them. This was humiliating in the extreme, and she prayed he wouldn't try anything else. The very thought of her neighbour pulling her panties down and gazing at her bared bottom was degradation beyond belief.

But she had little time to ponder her shame as the firm palm of his hand swept down to meet the sensitive flesh of her tensed buttocks with a loud retort. She couldn't suppress a yelp as she wondered what was happening to her life. How had she fallen into this dreadful situation?

Again the palm struck, landing squarely across the quivering globes, the stinging sensation permeating her flesh, her auburn hair hanging down, her face buried in the cushion of the chair's back to muffle her cries. A million thoughts battered her tormented mind as she waited for the next gruelling slap. This was her lounge, the family lounge, and she was bending over her father's favourite armchair with her knickers pulled down to her knees and her neighbour spanking her bare bottom; how could she be allowing this to happen?

'Please...' she whimpered as the man pinned her down with his free hand flat on the small of her back, and ignoring her cry for mercy, swept his spanking hand down again to impact loudly against her shuddering buttocks. Wondering how many agonising spanks she was to endure she felt tears welling in her eyes. Again the sound of flesh meeting flesh filled her ears, the slap of his palm reverberating around the lounge. 'No more,' she cried, gripping the arms of the chair. 'Please, Mr Price, no more.'

'All right,' he conceded, a little out of breath as he lowered his hand to his side. 'But remember this; while I am charged with looking after you, you will show me due respect and you will do as I say. Do you understand?'

'Yes, Mr Price,' she breathed shakily, and he nodded his satisfaction.

'Good, that's more like it.'

'May I stand up now, Mr Price?' she asked timorously, her sweet voice a little muffled by the back of the chair.

'No, not yet,' he refused. 'You took your spanking pretty well, so to show that I'm a considerate chap and fairly pleased with you, I'll massage some cooling cream into your bottom.'

'No,' she said, tensing at the thought of his hands mauling her, 'it's all right, Mr Price. You don't have to do that, thank you.'

'Nonsense, I've brought some cream with me,' he insisted. 'It'll soothe the sting from your bottom...'

Closing her eyes as she felt the cream against the burning flesh of her buttocks, Emily shuddered, but with the very thought of her next-door neighbour massaging it into her naked bottom making her cringe, she knew that she daren't protest. With his slick fingers slipping between the glowing cheeks she wondered what this was leading to, how far he was going to take the shameful violation of her body.

But then, biting her lip and clinging to the arms of the chair as his fingers moved dangerously close to the tiny star of her anus, she realised the sensations weren't at all unpleasant. With the cold cream extinguishing the fire in her buttocks and his slippery fingers teasing the secret valley between, she began to breathe more easily as her anxiety lessened, and as a rude fingertip fleetingly touched her anus she dared not object.

'You have a lovely bottom, Emily,' Arthur mumbled, massaging more cream into her rounded globes. 'Firm buttocks, perfectly symmetrical...'

'Thank you, but may I stand up now, Mr Price?' she breathed quietly.

'All in good time, my dear,' he replied pensively. 'All in good time. I must say, you are beginning to progress well after such a bad start. And I'm so pleased that I don't have to ring your parents.' Massaging the cream into the pink, blotchy handprints he'd created on her silky flesh, he moved down to her inner thighs. 'Is that nice?' he asked, his fingers transiently touching the pouting lips of her vulva and making her gasp.

'No...' she whispered confusedly, 'I mean, I'd like to stand up now please, Mr Price.'

There was a long, tense pause, and then Arthur bent and untied the bonds around her ankles. 'Yes, of course,' he said. 'And I think you'd better get yourself off to bed now.'

Chapter 6

Emily yawned, sat upright, stretched and rubbed her eyes, and looked around her bedroom. It was eight o'clock, another morning had arrived and stark reality returned.

Pushing the quilt back she slipped out of bed and went across the landing to the bathroom. With her buttocks still throbbing lightly from her spanking the night before, she took a hot shower, luxuriating in the steaming cascade of water, and having just dried herself the phone rang in her parents' bedroom and she hurried to answer it.

'Hi, Emily,' Christine regaled cheerfully. 'Want to come into town?'

'What happened when you came round?' Emily asked directly. 'I thought you were going to hide in the dining room until Arthur had gone? Wasn't the backdoor open?'

'The door was locked,' the girl told her. 'Emily, are you all right now?'

'No, no I'm not.'

'Why don't you come into town with me? It'll do you good to get out for a while.'

'Did you see Jack in the wine bar?'

'Yes, I did. He was in a bit of a mood. He said he'd been here but you'd gone out. He then waited in the bar for two hours for you to turn up.'

'You shouldn't have given him my address, Chrissie,' Emily told her friend. 'But anyway, I hadn't gone out. I was upstairs in my bedroom.'

'I don't know what this is all about, Emily, but I think you'd better meet me in town and we'll have a coffee and a chat. You obviously need to talk about this.'

'What's the point? You'd never believe me.'

'Well, I do find the things you've told me a bit difficult to believe,' Christine admitted a little sheepishly. 'Wouldn't you?'

'Yes, I suppose so,' Emily acknowledged begrudgingly.

'Well, are you coming into town?'

'Maybe.'

'I'll meet you in the coffee shop.'

'If I'm not there by ten-thirty come round here,' Emily said.

'Okay, I'll see you later.'

Replacing the receiver, Emily went back to her bedroom and dried her hair. Going into town with Christine, chatting and laughing in the coffee shop, planning their evenings out - that's what this two weeks should have been like, she reflected. Having fun and living for a change. But what, she pondered, slipping into a pair of white cotton panties, did she have to look forward to now?

Then putting on a pink cotton skirt and white T-shirt, she looked out of her window at the garden and the clear blue sky. It was going to be another lovely day, and promised to be too hot to bother with a bra.

Brushing her hair again in front of her dressing table mirror, she pondered how ridiculous it was to have to call her neighbour, and friend of the family, Mr

Price. When she was young she'd called him uncle, and that had progressed over the years to Arthur. To now call him Mr Price was daft, and feeling positive at the start of a new and glorious day, she decided she wouldn't do it. He'd started to take her along a path to she knew not where, but she wasn't taking another step.

Leaving the house by the backdoor as the time neared nine, she took a deep breath to calm her apprehension as she walked along the alleyway into Arthur's back garden. She'd have it out with him, and then go into town to meet Christine.

'Ah, there you are,' the man said as Emily wandered through the open door into his kitchen.

'Good morning,' she said pleasantly, but her optimism evaporated as she saw how stern he looked. 'It's going to be hot today,' she added conversationally.

'I'm not interested in the weather, Emily,' he returned, closing the backdoor and turning the key in the lock.

'Wouldn't it be best to let the breeze come through—?'

'What were your thoughts when you went to bed last night?' he suddenly demanded, right out of the blue.

'My thoughts?' she echoed, frowning in puzzlement. 'When I went to bed?'

'Yes, Emily, what were you thinking about as you lay in your bed.'

'I wasn't thinking about anything in particular, Mr Price.' Her resolve not to call him that dissolved in the face of his brusque interrogation.

'Weren't you?'

'No, not really, I went straight to sleep.'

He shook his head and tutted. 'Why do you persist in lying, Emily?'

'Um, lying?' She forced a laugh and nervously brushed her auburn hair away from her brow. 'Why would I be lying?'

'Mr Price,' he prompted.

'Mr Price.'

'Come through to the lounge, Emily. We need to talk.'

Following him along the hall she wondered what he wanted now and then followed his unspoken direction to sit on his sofa, while he stood with his back to the lounge window, shaking his head disapprovingly.

'What is it?' she finally ventured to ask, becoming increasingly uneasy. 'What am I supposed to have done wrong now?'

'Mr Price.'

She huffed in exasperation. 'What am I supposed to have done wrong now, *Mr Price?*'

'You went to bed last night, and...?' he prompted.

'I... I don't understand...' she said without conviction, fearful that she was beginning to understand only too well.

'You went to bed and masturbated again, Emily,' he stated.

'No,' she gasped, holding her hand to her open mouth. 'I... I...'

'Don't deny it. You went to bed and masturbated, didn't you?'

This was ridiculous, she thought. She was sure he was guessing as he stared accusingly at her. How could he have known what she'd been doing in the privacy of her bed? He *was* guessing. He had to be. 'No, I did not,' she insisted. 'But if I did it would be no business of yours. What I do in the privacy of my home is *my* business.'

'And your parents',' he corrected. 'Is this how you intend to carry on when they get back?'

'I did *not* masturbate last night,' she stated firmly. 'I did *not* masturbate. Mr Price.'

'I heard you, Emily,' he informed her coldly, dropping the bombshell with perfect timing. 'Through the wall, I could hear every whimper, every disgusting gasp of sexual gratification.'

Lowering her eyes, her cheeks flushing pink, Emily was sure he couldn't have heard her; the walls weren't that thin. But on the other hand he was right, she *had* masturbated, and somehow he'd discovered her secret. Was there nothing she could do without his knowledge? There'd been no privacy in her home since Arthur had taken control, and now, even beneath her quilt, there was no escaping the man's prying.

'As I said to you the other day, I have nothing against masturbation,' he said. 'But to carry on masturbating when you know your father has seen you, when you know how distressed he was—'

'Oh, just shut up!' Emily snapped impetuously, standing up and moving to the lounge door. 'You've threatened to tell my parents this and that, you've threatened to ruin their holiday, I've had enough of this. As far as I'm concerned you can go to hell!'

'Do your parents know what you've done?' he asked her mysteriously, making her stop in the hall and spin round.

'What do you mean?' she asked.

'If your parents discovered your dreadful secret they'd throw you out of the house.'

Her head spinning, Emily didn't know what he was talking about. Dreadful secret? Her father had already discovered her masturbating, there could be nothing worse than that, so what did Arthur mean? Had he dreamed up some fantastic story about her? What had he written in the report book? What photographs had he doctored?

Returning in defeat to the lounge she sat back down on the sofa and gazed up at him, his expression one of triumph.

'When I spanked you last night,' he went on, eyeing the tiny triangle of white cotton panties just visible beneath her skirt. 'When I pulled your panties down and spanked you, do you know what I saw, Emily?'

'W-what do you mean?' she stammered.

'Do your parents know what you've done?' he again asked her.

Her breathing fast and shallow, her anxiety rising, Emily held her hand to her head. When Arthur had pulled her panties down to her knees, in the grip of humiliation she'd forgotten about her secret.

Biting her lip, she knew that if her father discovered the existence of the small tattoo on the upper slope of her right buttock he'd be absolutely furious. He hated tattoos on men, but on women it was simply intolerable.

Defacing the body was, in his mind, akin to blasphemy. In his view a girl with a tattoo was nothing but a jezebel, a cheap strumpet, and now Emily's secret was out.

Recalling the time she'd gone to the tattoo artist with a group of girls from the Uni, she wished she'd made a stand against having one done. But they laughed at her, taunted her, and finally goaded her into agreeing to have the tattoo. She'd wanted to be like the others, she reflected. She only wanted to be accepted as one of the gang. Had her father not been so strict... no, she could not blame her father.

'In answer to your question,' she said shakily, 'yes, my parents do know.'

'Another lie,' Arthur countered confidently. 'Lies, deceit, insubordination; is there no end to your wickedness?'

'Arthur, can't we—?'

'I was hoping you'd not force me to mention the tattoo. It was obviously your secret and, understanding as I am, I wanted to leave it that way.'

'You can't tell my parents, Arthur,' she beseeched. 'Please, I'm begging you not to tell them.'

With a sadistic glint in his eyes, Arthur took his time scrutinising her as she sat uneasily on the sofa. Emily didn't know what to say, what to do. The tattoo had been a stupid mistake, something she'd bitterly regretted ever since having it done. But it was no good looking back. What was done was done. Arthur had such a hold on her now that she was totally in his hands.

'What... what do you want?' Emily asked uncomfortably. 'Isn't it about time you told me?'

'I think it's too late,' he sighed, shaking his head as though with deep regret. 'I was hoping to help make a fine young
woman out of you, and...'

'And what?'

'Perhaps there's still time.'

'What do you mean?'

'I'm not going to give up on you, Emily,' he announced. 'I didn't realise how badly behaved you are, but I set out to make something of you and I'm not going to give up now. No, I'm going to change things.'

'Change what?' she asked timorously, not liking the way this was going.

'I'm going to change tack,' he told her. 'You go into town and enjoy a coffee and some time with your friend.'

Emily stared at Arthur. 'How did you know I'd arranged to meet Christine?' she asked.

'She rang me earlier.'

'Christine wouldn't ring you,' Emily argued. 'How or why would she know your number?'

'Whether you believe that she would or wouldn't is beside the point,' he said casually. 'She rang me because she's worried about you, and with good reason, too. Go to the coffee shop as you'd arranged and I'll prepare the room for you.'

'The room?' she echoed. 'What room?'

'You'll see, Emily,' he said mysteriously. 'You'll see.'

Leaving while she had the chance, Emily wondered whether Arthur had somehow been eavesdropping on her phone conversation. There was no way Christine would ring him, she reflected. She didn't really know the man, let alone his phone number, but how could he know about their arrangements?

Going back into her house to get her little shoulder bag, she noticed her trembling fingers. She was becoming a nervous wreck, she thought, clenching her fists and taking a deep breath. Arthur was slowly and systematically wearing her down.

Just then the front doorbell rang, making her jump and immediately admonish herself for being so twitchy. She went to the front door, and breathed a huge sigh of relief as she opened it and saw the beaming face of her best friend there.

'What's the matter?' Christine asked, wandering into the lounge.

'Everything,' Emily replied. 'Thank goodness you're here.'

'I didn't think you'd go to the coffee shop, so I came to see what's up.'

'Christine, you have to help me,' Emily blurted. 'I'm going to leave home.'

'Great,' the girl grinned. 'We'll get a flat together.'

Emily shook her head. 'No, no you don't understand. I don't have any money.'

'Then how are you going to leave home?'

'That's just it, I don't know. Your parents have a spare room, don't they?'

'Well yes, but...'

'It's Arthur,' Emily sighed. 'He's... oh, I don't know where to start. Did you phone him this morning?'

'Phone your next-door neighbour?' Christine giggled. 'No, of course I didn't. Why would I? *How* could I? I don't have his number.'

Emily's brow furrowed. 'I thought as much,' she mused.

'What's going on, Emily?'

'Arthur has been disciplining me,' she disclosed. 'By that I mean he's spanked me, tied me with rope, chained me up like a dog, thrashed me with a leather belt...'

'You what?' Christine gasped incredulously.

'You don't believe me, do you?'

'I'm not saying you're lying,' Christine said noncommittally. 'It's just that these are incredible accusations.'

'My parents asked Arthur to keep an eye on me,' Emily explained.

'Yes, you told me.'

'I've always looked upon Arthur as a friend of the family - as an uncle, almost - and didn't think he'd... he has a front door key and a backdoor key,' she finished, as though that explained all.

'Go on,' Christine urged.

'When I get in at night, he's waiting for me.'

'Here, in your house?'

'Yes, he's always lurking, checking up on me, spying on me,' she confided to her friend. 'You won't believe this, Chrissie, but he has a report book in which he fills in the time I go out, when I get back, and all sorts of comments about me. I really don't know what to do.'

'What?' Christine snorted. 'That sounds crazy.'

'He even has photographs of me.'

'Photographs?'

'Here,' Emily said, pulling the envelope out from beneath the sofa. 'You see?'

'Shit, you're not lying,' Christine breathed incredulously. 'But why is he doing this?'

'Because he's a creep,' Emily said with passion. 'But there's worse - he knows about my tattoo.'

'What tattoo?' Christine asked, shocked.

'This tattoo,' Emily said, lifting her skirt, lowering the waistband of her panties a little, and turning. 'See?'

'I didn't know you had that,' Christine said with admiration. 'You're a dark horse, Ems. When did you have it done, and more to the point, how did Arthur get to see it?'

'When he spanked me,' Emily said. 'So do you believe me now?'

'Yep, and you'll be staying with us until your parents get back,' Christine said, giving her answer.

'Thanks, Chrissie.' Emily sighed with relief. 'I can't stay here, that's for sure.'

Having arranged to see her friend at her house as soon as she'd gathered together a few changes of clothing and essentials, she saw her out and was just turning to go upstairs to pack when she froze with dread.

'This is most disappointing,' Arthur said, standing in the kitchen doorway. 'Why do you want to stay at Christine's house?'

'I-I don't,' Emily stammered, forcing an unconvincing smile.

'You're intending to stay at her house until your parents get back from holiday.'

'No, I—'

'After all we've talked about, you're still lying.'

'I'm not.'

'Before you bother to dream up some story or other, I'd better tell you that I was listening. Can you imagine your parents' reaction if they were to hear that you'd left home?'

'I'm not leaving home,' she objected.

'They go on holiday to Spain, and you decide to move out while they're away?'

'Arthur, I am not planning to move out.'

'Mr Price, if you please,' he said sharply. 'This continuing poor behaviour is no good, Emily. It is no good at all, which is why I've just been talking to your father on the phone.'

'What?' Her head spinning, she held her hands to her open mouth. 'You rang him?'

'I had no choice,' he said matter-of-factly. 'You have to understand the position I'm in. The position *you've* put me in.'

'Are they coming home?' she asked fretfully. 'What did you tell him? What did he say?'

'I had to be honest with him, of course,' he said smoothly. 'I didn't tell him everything, but I had to tell him that you'd come home late on three occasions.' He smiled without warmth. 'Be fair, Emily, what else could I do?'

'But I thought we had an agreement,' she said despairingly.

'So did I,' he concurred. 'I thought we'd agreed that you weren't going to lie any more. I thought you were going to behave as you should. I thought you were going to call me Mr Price.'

'Why should I call you Mr Price?' she challenged.

'Because it's an important part of your education.'

'Education? You were asked to keep an eye on me, not educate me.'

'And that's what I am going to do, Emily,' he vowed ominously. 'I am going to help you become an obedient, respectable young lady. And for starters, your father has forbidden you to go out at all in the evenings for the remainder of their time away. He agrees with me that you can't be trusted.'

'But—'

'There are no buts. He stated in no uncertain terms that you are not to go out in the evenings.'

'This is ridiculous,' Emily said indignantly. 'I'm eighteen years old.'

'So you keep saying.'

'What else did you tell my father?'

'I've not been telling tales, Emily,' he insisted. 'I phoned him because I was worried about you. This is your doing, so don't blame me for the way you've behaved.'

'You shouldn't have phoned him.'

'How can you say that when you've planned to move out?'

'I haven't planned to move out.'

'So you're not going to stay at Christine's house?'

Emily lowered her eyes and shook her head.

'I beg your pardon, I couldn't hear you.'

'No, Mr Price,' she whispered dejectedly, her eyes sparkling with unshed tears as she looked back up at him.

'Good.' He looked satisfied. 'Now, I have some work to be getting on with. I'm preparing a little surprise for you.'

'What is it?' she asked, her eyes wide with uncertainty.

'You'll see,' he said enigmatically. 'And by the way, in future you won't answer the front door. I don't want you talking to Christine and getting silly ideas. And you won't answer the phone, either.'

Chapter 7

It would be a mistake to go to Christine's house, Emily decided as she sat on the bench in the park and gazed at the kids playing on the swings. Arthur would not only have seen her leave the house, but possibly even followed her. Was he lurking in the bushes or behind a tree with his digital camera? He wasn't far away, she sensed that much.

'Hi,' someone called, and Emily turned and stared at the young man there. 'How are you?'

'Jack,' she gasped, anxiously scanning the park for a sighting of her neighbour. 'What are you doing here?'

'I'm on my way home,' he replied. 'It's great to see you.'

'Jack, you must go.'

'Why?' He looked puzzled.

'Please, just go.'

'Oh I get it,' he said with a sneer. 'You don't want to know me.'

'No, no, it's not that,' she said hastily.

'Then what is it?'

'I can't explain. Just go, please.'

'Emily, I've been messed around before and I don't want to be again. You've already stood me up once, so it's pretty obvious you don't want to see me.'

'I do, Jack,' Emily insisted. 'I really do want to see you.'

'So?' he said, sitting beside her on the bench. 'So what's the problem?'

'I can't be seen here with you.'

'Have you got a boyfriend?' he asked her, turning and looking around the park. 'Are you waiting for him? Is that it?'

'No, no, I don't have a boyfriend,' she maintained.

'You're not married, are you?'

'No!'

Offering him a smile as he brushed his unruly black hair away from his suntanned face, Emily felt her stomach somersault. He was good-looking, she thought, remembering their kiss. Wearing faded blue jeans and a white shirt, his dark eyes sparkling, he returned her smile, and Emily was desperate to get to know him better.

As he leaned forward and kissed her lips, Emily inhaled his male scent and felt as though she was drifting on clouds of euphoria. Her eyes closed as he finally moved away, and she let out a dreamy sigh of satisfaction.

'Be honest, Emily,' he said, his hand venturing to rest on hers, 'if you don't want to know me then just say so.'

'But I do,' she whispered, acutely aware of her nipples brushing against the material of her T-shirt. 'I've given you my phone number, haven't I?'

'You've given me *a* number,' he agreed. 'But is it any old number just to get rid of me?'

'It's *my* phone number, Jack. Look, you must go now. I can't explain, but I will when I next see you.'

'I'll ring you.'

'Yes, do that. Jack, I really do like you.'

'I'll ring you,' he repeated, getting up from the bench.

'Jack, I do want to see you.'

'Yeah, I know.'

Watching him walk across the grass, Emily felt deflated. Would he ring? She'd made a mess of it, she knew as she watched him grow smaller in the distance. She should have convinced him how much she wanted to see him again. She should have, but it was too late now. He was walking out of her life, and it was Arthur's fault...

'What are you doing here?' That very man's voice broke into her sullen daydream, making her jump. He was standing behind her.

'What are *you* doing here?' she responded. Had he seen her talking to Jack? Had he seen her *kissing* Jack? 'Is there no getting away from you for five minutes?'

'Getting away from me?' he said, moving around the bench to stand before her. He was holding his small digital camera. 'I merely came out for a walk on such a glorious day as this and happened to see you here.'

'Happened to see me?' she said with some sarcasm. 'Don't you mean you followed me here and hid in the bushes spying on me?'

'No, I mean what I said,' he insisted. 'And very lucky that I did, too, for I was able to gather some more evidence of your extremely questionable behaviour, young lady.' He indicated the camera. 'I saw you with that lout.'

'I was only—'

'Allowing him to kiss you?' He paused, watching her, waiting for a denial, but none came. 'Exactly,' he concluded, nodding.

'Please, Mr Price,' Emily sighed in exasperation, 'I've asked you this countless times, but what is it you want from me? And please don't just say discipline and obedience.'

'I do want discipline and obedience, Emily,' he confirmed again. 'But I also want to play a major role in your life.'

'A major role? What do you mean by that?'

'Well, Emily, I look upon myself as your guardian,' he explained. 'You see, an attractive girl like you let loose is likely to get herself into trouble, as you've just proved.'

'I bumped into Jack and we talked for a few minutes,' she told him, 'that's all.'

'Talked?' he scoffed. 'Is that what you call it? Behaving indecently in public is nearer the truth.'

'And I haven't been let loose in the park,' she went on resentfully. 'I'm not a dog that's escaped from its leash.'

'Maybe you should be on a leash, Emily,' he pondered. 'Maybe you should be chained to the radiator until your parents return.'

'I beg your pardon?' Emily couldn't believe what she was hearing.

'I didn't want you to leave the house today because I knew what you'd do. And I was right.'

'Right about what?' she challenged. 'What did I do?'

'You came straight to the park, met that young hooligan and behaved in a decidedly lewd manner with him, in public.'

'Lewd manner?' Emily was incredulous. 'But we only kissed.'

'You see,' he said, with a smugness that made her feel as though her words were a confession, 'you even admit it. You can't be trusted and you're not capable of keeping yourself out of trouble. That's why you need me to look after you, young lady. That's why you need me as your guardian.'

'But I don't need you as a guardian,' she argued as he sat beside her on the bench. 'I don't need *anyone* as a guardian. I'm perfectly capable of looking after myself, thank you very much.'

Arthur tutted and shook his head as though amused by her independent stance. 'Of course you do,' he said. 'You're only out of my sight for five minutes and I find you canoodling with some young yob.' He smiled broadly, placing his hand on her knee and giving it a little squeeze. 'Now,' he said, 'how do you fancy doing some modelling for me?'

'Modelling for you?' Emily was perplexed.

'Yes,' he nodded. 'I love using my camera - as you know by now - so why don't I take some more nice photos of you?'

Emily frowned uncertainly. 'Oh, I'm not so sure—'

'Yes,' he went on without listening to her, 'we'll have a little photographic session in your garden. It'll be fun. Come on, let's go shall we?'

Emily knew the last was a rhetorical question, so following Arthur across the park she pondered the realisation that she was beginning to obey his every word and accept his demands and treatment of her with little resistance. It was all becoming the norm; how things were; Arthur snapped his fingers and she jumped.

Arriving home they went through the back gate into her garden. 'Oh yes, this is perfect,' Arthur enthused, taking the lens cap off his camera. 'We not only have the sunshine, but privacy too.'

'Shall I sit here?' Emily suggested, pointing to a patio chair, wanting to get the charade over with quickly.

'No, no,' he said, gazing around for inspiration. 'I think we'll have you standing beneath the apple tree first.'

'What are you going to do with the photos?' she asked, following him to the shady area beneath the branches.

'I told you, they're for my private collection,' he said. 'Now, lean casually against the trunk.'

Doing so, Emily knew Arthur was taking shots up her skirt as he settled on the ground, and although completely against her normal instincts, she was actually enjoying posing for him, and even more strangely, enjoying knowing the camera lens could catch teasing glimpses of her knickers. In front of the camera she suddenly felt carefree. The threats, the coercion, the spanking, the fear of her father discovering her apparent wickedness, all seemed to fade away. Posing for the camera made her feel like a model, made her feel beautiful and feminine. She had a good body, she knew, placing her free hand on her hip. Recalling photographs she'd seen in magazines, she tossed her auburn hair over her shoulder and looked up at the glorious azure sky through the shady branches. For the first time in ages she felt good, she felt relaxed.

'That's lovely,' Arthur encouraged. 'Now, just lift your skirt up a little more...'

'Hiya,' Christine called cheerfully, appearing through the back gate.

'Oh, er... hi,' Emily said, lowering her arm and moving away from the tree.

'I thought you might want to come for a walk,' Christine said, looking curiously at Arthur and the camera.

'I'm not sure,' Emily said, glancing at Arthur and then back at her friend.

'No, you've already been out for a walk,' her neighbour brusquely answered for her, straightening up and casting the intruder a look of disdain. 'Why don't you come back in an hour or so, young lady?' he suggested.

'Is that all right with you, Ems?' Christine asked, frowning quizzically at her friend.

'Yes, yes,' Emily nodded, not wanting to incur any more of the man's wrath, 'come back in an hour.'

'Okay,' she agreed. 'Oh, by the way,' she added, 'my father's coming round to see you later, Ems.'

'Oh, that's good,' Emily said, trying to play down the announcement and hoping Christine wouldn't risk dropping her in further trouble by saying any more.

'He needs to see you, if you get my meaning...' Christine added cryptically. 'Right, I'll be going, and I'll see you in a little while.'

Waiting until the girl had left, Arthur took Emily's hand and led her into the house, locked the backdoor and immediately ushered her into the lounge. 'You see the trouble you've caused now?' he said sternly.

'What trouble?' Emily asked timorously; was she in for another spanking, or a beating with the belt?

'This idea of yours to move out,' he said, 'just now we're getting on so well together. Now your meddling friend and her father are sticking their noses in and you've spoiled everything.'

'He only wants to see me,' she said unconvincingly.

'Why would he want to see you?' he probed. 'Why did she say, "if you get my meaning"?'

'I don't know,' she said. 'I've always got on well with her father, so...'

'You get on with him, do you?' he said thoughtfully.

'Yes, I do,' Emily confirmed. 'I mean, I've known him since I was at school. He's a very nice man.'

'I see,' Arthur said, rubbing his chin. 'And how often has he been round to see you?'

'How often?' Emily was feeling increasingly uncomfortable being interrogated like this. 'I don't really know.'

'Has he come to see you when your parents have been out?'

'Yes, they've been out on the odd occasion when Dave's called.'

'Oh, Dave, is it?' Arthur looked distinctly put out by what he was hearing.

'Yes,' Emily nodded, 'that's his name.'

'Your friend Christine knows about this, and she condones it?' he pressed.

'Condones what?' Emily asked, baffled by the direction of his questioning. 'I don't know what you're suggesting, but—'

'I think you know very well what I'm suggesting, Emily,' he snapped. 'Don't start your lying again.'

'Lying?' she gasped. 'Lying about what? All I said was that Christine's father has been here and—'

'How old is he?'

'How old? I don't know. In his forties, I suppose. What's that got to do with anything?'

Arthur shook his head menacingly. 'I'm shocked, young lady,' he said. 'He's more than twice your age.'

'Yes, I know. What are you getting at? Sometimes Dave comes here and—'

'There's no need to go into the sordid details,' Arthur cut in angrily.

'Sordid?'

'A man in his forties? Your best friend's father? Have you no morals?'

'What do you mean?' Emily shrieked. 'Are you suggesting that I... that I...?'

'I'm going to have to speak with Christine's mother,' Arthur vowed. 'I really had no idea you'd fallen so low. I'm lost for words, Emily. Completely lost for words.'

Arthur had the uncanny knack of turning a perfectly innocent situation into something tacky, Emily reflected. And even worse, he had the uncanny knack of making her feel guilty when she wasn't! To even think that she had something going with Christine's father was obscene. She liked Dave, that was true, but anything more than that was unthinkable. She'd known him and Christine's mother since she'd met her long-term friend at junior school, and always respected them as the parents of her friend. If Arthur talked to Christine's mother there'd be serious ramifications for sure, she knew.

'When did all this start?' Arthur asked.

'Nothing has started,' Emily returned. 'To suggest that something has been going on between Christine's father and me is disgusting.'

'You're right, young lady,' he concurred, 'it is disgusting. So much has come to light since your parents went away, and with every revelation I am increasingly horrified.'

'Nothing's come to light,' Emily disagreed.

'Nothing?' Arthur laughed derisively. 'Never in a million years would I have believed you could behave so abominably.'

'I am not behaving abominably,' she argued.

'I'd always thought you to be a quiet, refined, decent girl, but the shocking truth is, well, just that; shocking. I could possibly understand you having some sort of relationship with youths of your own age, but with a married man old enough to be your father?'

'I am not having a relationship with anyone,' Emily snapped. 'Your mind is disgusting, it's riddled with filth.'

'My mind is riddled with thoughts of your disgusting behaviour, Emily,' he said. 'So yes, you're right; my mind is riddled with thoughts of *your* filth. Why are you like this? Where on earth did your parents go wrong?'

'They didn't go wrong,' she sobbed, tears threatening to burst forth. 'I've never done anything with Christine's father... or anyone else for that matter.'

'It's no good putting on the waterworks, Emily,' he said without compassion. 'You can't get round me like that.'

'Why are you doing this to me?' she beseeched. 'Why are you causing all this trouble for me?'

'There you go with your nonsense again,' he snorted. 'Why am I causing all this trouble? I didn't tell you to go to the park and meet that thug. I didn't tell you to put on a shameful display with him by kissing and canoodling in public.'

'Please,' she whimpered, wiping tears from her eyes. 'Please, leave me alone.'

'It's not me who should be leaving you alone, Emily,' he went on relentlessly. 'It's that thug. It's your friend's father. It's whoever else you're carrying on with without me or your parents knowing '

'I am not carrying on with anyone,' she protested.

'From now on you're not to leave this house without my say so,' he decreed, ignoring her assertion. 'Do you understand me?'

Emily shook her head in bewilderment, her eyes sparkling with tears.

'All right, have it your own way,' he said ominously. 'I know Christine's surname and address so I'll look up her number and ring her mother,' he announced, leaving the lounge.

Hearing the backdoor slam shut, Emily flopped onto the sofa and despondently held her head in her hands. If Arthur spoke to Christine's mother all hell would break loose. She recalled Christine's revelation of a year before. Her parents were having marital problems. It had something to do with her father seeing another woman. Christine said it wasn't true, but the seeds of doubt had been sown in her mother's mind. Christine's father was very good-looking, and according to Christine, he had an eye for the ladies. Emily wasn't sure how the problems had started, but she recalled something about Dave giving a female colleague a lift home one evening. Christine had said it was nothing, but her mother was suspicious when she heard that her husband had been seen in a pub with the woman. So if spiteful Arthur told Christine's mother that her husband had something going on with Emily, well, she dreaded to think what might happen. Although innocent, Emily recalled one of her father's sayings: if enough mud is thrown some of it will stick. This was a time bomb just waiting to explode...

Emily jumped as the phone rang. She dashed into the hall and lifted the receiver to her ear. 'Hello?' she gasped.

'Emily,' Christine began conspiratorially, 'Arthur's just phoned.'

'God, no,' Emily panted anxiously. 'What did he want?'

'He wanted to talk to my mother. What's going on?'

'What did your mother say?'

'Nothing. She's out shopping. Arthur told me not to come round to your house for a while because you have to concentrate on your studying. And he said your parents don't want you to stay round here with me.'

'Is he going to call your mother when she gets back?' Emily asked fearfully.

'I don't know. All he said was that he'd spoken to your father and you're not allowed to stay round here while they're on holiday, and I'm not to come round to your place.'

'Is your dad there?'

'He was, but he's gone out.'

'Does he know Arthur rang?'

'Yes, I told him,' her friend confirmed. 'He's worried about you, Ems. He's going to call round to speak to you.'

'No, no he mustn't,' Emily said desperately.

'Why ever not?'

'I can't talk about it on the phone. What have you told him, exactly?'

'Just that you want to move in here until your parents get home. I didn't tell him about Arthur spanking you and stuff because, well, to be honest he'd never believe me.'

'Ring him on his mobile, Chrissie,' Emily told her friend, her mind racing. 'He mustn't come round here. Ring him, okay?'

'Okay, okay, if that's what you want,' Christine said in a placatory tone. 'I'll call you back once I've spoken to him.'

'Yes, yes do that, please.' Replacing the receiver, Emily sat on the stairs and lowered her head. She was in a complete and utter mess. How had it come to this?

Chapter 8

Emily obediently stayed home for the rest of the day. Despondent and fearful, she couldn't believe that Arthur had accused her of having an affair with Christine's father. The very notion was ludicrous and insulting, to both of them.

With dusk falling she was relieved that Dave hadn't been to see her, and she guessed that Christine had managed to contact him on his mobile and head him off. But why hadn't her friend called back to confirm that - to stop her worrying so much?

Thankfully there'd been no sign of Arthur, either. Things were very quiet, almost too quiet, which worried Emily as well. She'd at least expected him to check up on her.

Having paced the lounge for what seemed like hours, she froze as she heard Arthur's front door close. He was coming to see her, she was sure as she gazed apprehensively out of the lounge window. He was coming round to see her again. Now what did he want? What cruel games did he intend to play on her this time?

But watching from the window she saw him climb into his car and drive off. She frowned. Was he going to see Christine's mother to cause trouble? Wherever he was going, Emily hoped he'd be gone long enough to give her time to slip into his house and retrieve the evidence he'd gathered against her. Knowing time was of the essence, without thinking in case she lost her nerve, she slipped out of the backdoor and crept along the alley into Arthur's garden. This was dangerous, but she had to do it. Relieved to find his backdoor unlocked, she looked over her shoulder at his garden before going inside. Was this a trap? Had he parked down the street and crept back along the alleyway to catch her doing exactly what she was doing? Deciding it was too late for such doubts, she stole into his kitchen and closed the door behind her. Had he forgotten to lock up, or *was* this a trap?

Convincing herself she'd have time to flee the house if she heard his car pulling up outside in the street, she climbed the stairs to his office at the front of the house. The place was quiet, creepy. Opening the office door she saw his computer. She'd have to get into the files and locate the photographs, she knew, switching it on. The printed photographs would be somewhere here, and she opened the top drawer of the desk and rummaged through a pile of papers. Not expecting anyone to search his office, Arthur would believe there to be no reason to stash the evidence in a safer place.

Bundled together in a neat pile, the pictures of her lay in the bottom of the drawer. She'd done it! 'Yes!' she whispered, congratulating herself and grabbing the photos. With her heart racing, adrenalin coursing through her veins, she couldn't believe she'd got her hands on the incriminating evidence. She again wondered if this was a trick, scanning the street below for any sign of Arthur's return, wondering if he'd intentionally lured her into his house. Was it a plan for him to come back, catch her stealing from his office and thereby create an excuse to punish her again?

Knowing it was too late to let such thoughts distract her, she sat at his desk and searched through his computer files. Again unable to believe her luck as she came across a file named *Emily*, she clicked the delete button. The computer asked if she really wanted to do that, and grinning victoriously she confirmed that she did. That was that, she thought, emptying the recycle bin and switching the computer off. Now Arthur had nothing on her. Now Arthur could go to hell.

Clutching her spoils and hastily returning to her house, she sat on the sofa and flicked through the photographs. To her horror she discovered that Arthur had clearly been taking many when she wasn't even aware of it. What a slime-bag!

Deciding to burn them all later that night, she stuffed them beneath the sofa. All Arthur had on her now was her tattoo and the report book. Without the photos his so-called evidence against her was pretty flimsy. The tables were beginning to turn in her favour, she sensed, but there was still the problem of Christine's father.

'Emily,' Arthur called, walking along the garden path to the open backdoor, 'have you been round to my house?'

'Many times,' she replied, playing dumb as she went through to the kitchen.

'No, this evening I mean,' he clarified.

Emily shook her head. 'You'd have seen me.'

'I had to go out. Are you sure you didn't? If you're lying you know what you'll get.'

'Of course I'm sure,' she said, feeling more positive than she had for a while. 'I'd know if I'd been round to your house, wouldn't I?'

'Mr Price, Emily, and don't forget it,' he corrected her angrily, clearly uncomfortable with her newfound confidence. 'I've been speaking to Christine's mother,' he revealed with a triumphant leer. 'We had quite a chat.'

'Oh?'

'About you and her husband. She was most interested.'

'I'm sure she was.'

'You don't seem particularly concerned,' he observed.

'Why should I be concerned? You're free to chat to anyone you like.'

'Yes but, this was about you having an affair with her husband.'

'And? It's not true so why should it bother me? Now if you don't mind I'd like to have a soak in the bath and get an early night.'

'This is most regrettful,' Arthur sighed, leaving the kitchen and heading for the lounge. 'Most regretful indeed.'

Raising her eyes to the ceiling, Emily knew she was supposed to follow him and ask what he meant. But then again she didn't have to play his games any more, did she? He might have discovered his photographs were missing, but as long as she kept to her story and denied going to his house, she'd be all right. He'd know it was her, of course, but he couldn't prove it and there'd be little or nothing he could do. The tables *were* turning, and formulating an idea she wandered into the lounge and smiled at him.

'Come to think of it,' she said, 'I did hear a noise a little earlier.'

'A noise?'

'Yes, coming from your place. I assumed it was you and didn't think anything of it. I also heard mumbled voices. Two men, I think.'

'Two men?'

Emily nodded, warming to her tale. 'That's what it sounded like. I thought you must have a visitor. Oh no,' she said with exaggerated concern, 'you haven't been burgled, have you?'

'Not as far as I know.' His brooding eyes stared accusingly at her as he rubbed his chin. 'It's just that I'd left a book on the kitchen table, and when I got home it had been moved.'

'It has nothing to do with me,' Emily said gleefully. 'Now could you go, please?'

'Mr Price, Emily,' he reminded her, 'and don't you forget it. Otherwise you'll be in line for another sound spanking.'

'Oh, I think not,' she countered, grinning confidently, thinking of the deleted folder and the photos hidden under her sofa.

'You think not, do you?' he said. 'I don't like your tone, young lady. Bend over and hold your ankles.'

'No, I won't,' she said defiantly. 'What a stupid thing to tell me to do.'

'Oh dear,' he mused, 'this is most regretful.'

'So you keep saying.' She felt like goading him, like pushing her luck a bit. Unable to stop herself grinning as Arthur walked to the lounge door, she knew she was winning - she was gaining the upper hand. Without the photos Arthur's grip on her was weakening. Her only problem now was her tattoo. The report book didn't bother her; Christine would give her an alibi; she'd confirm that they'd stayed in during the evenings to study together, making Arthur out to be the liar he obviously was. But the tattoo was a different matter.

'Most regretful, but I suspect you're tired so on this occasion I'll show some leniency,' Arthur went on. 'But if you speak to me like that again you'd better be prepared for the thrashing of your young life.'

'I think not,' Emily again said.

'Oh, I almost forgot,' he added, almost as an afterthought, reaching into his inside jacket pocket. 'This is for you.'

Emily's triumphant expression froze on her face as she looked at the object in his hand. 'A CD?' she muttered, taking the disc. 'What's on it?'

'I know you don't have a computer,' he said conversationally, 'but I thought you might like a copy of all the photos I've taken of you.'

'A copy?' she echoed, her stomach sinking. 'You mean, you have more copies of them?'

He chuckled. 'But of course, it's only sensible. If my computer crashed and I lost everything I have on my hard-drive it would be a disaster,' he explained patronisingly, as though talking to a child. 'Now, I'll say goodnight and see you in the morning.'

Feeling utterly deflated and numb as her tormentor disappeared next door, her hopes cruelly dashed, Emily realised he'd deliberately left his backdoor unlocked when he'd gone out. He knew she'd try to retrieve the evidence. Why else give her a CD now, of all times? He'd planned this, she was sure. He'd deliberately built up her hopes, and was now delighting in smashing them down again.

Impulsively dashing into the hall she slipped the catch up on the front door. Arthur wasn't going to creep into the house during the night, she'd make sure of that. Jamming a chair beneath the backdoor handle again, securing the house as best she could, she went upstairs to her room and sat on her bed.

This was a never-ending nightmare, she thought, pulling her T-shirt over her head and off. There really was no winning with the man. Day by day his grip on her was progressively tightening, and there was nothing she could do about it.

Wondering whether he really had spoken to Christine's mother as she stood and eased her skirt down her legs, stepped out of it, and tossed it onto the chair, she slipped her panties off and lay on top of her quilt.

Christine would have phoned, surely. If Arthur had been to see her mother and caused trouble, Christine would have told her.

Tossing and turning, Emily drifted in and out of sleep until the morning came. The sun streaming in through the window, warming her naked body, she propped herself up on her elbows and looked around her bedroom. Thankful that she'd barricaded the front and backdoor, she knew Arthur would be demanding that she let him in before long.

About to swing her legs off the bed and take a shower, she felt something touch the back of her thigh. Sitting upright and throwing the quilt to the side, she stared in horror at the pink vibrator lying there.

'No,' she gasped, realising that Arthur must have been in her room during the night. But how did he get into the house? Gazing dumbfounded at the cylindrical device, she reckoned he must have climbed in through a window. But the windows had been closed. Getting out of bed and hurrying downstairs she checked the front door. The latch was still up. Dashing through the hall to the kitchen she saw the chair still jammed beneath the handle of the backdoor. This was crazy. How, she pondered as she moved the chair and placed it back under the kitchen table, had he broken into her house?

Wandering into the lounge, she froze. Lying on the coffee table were several photographs of her naked and sprawled out on her quilt, and examining the pictures with mounting horror, she eyed the pink vibrator nestling between her parted thighs. How Arthur had managed to get in and take them didn't matter. What did matter was that he now had more incriminating evidence of shameful behaviour against her.

Tossing the photographs onto the table she felt she was becoming a puppet to the man. He was controlling her; he was her master. Unable to escape him, unable even to sleep in her own bed without him imposing upon her privacy, she was very much her neighbour's plaything. She was trapped. Should she give up any hope of ever leading a normal life again? What hope was there now of ever being free of his clutches?

Miserably climbing the stairs she went into the bathroom, and having locked the door, she hoped she could at least take a shower in peace.

'Tea or coffee?' Arthur called up from the kitchen.

'What?' Emily gasped, stopping on the landing between the bathroom and her bedroom, wrapped only in a fluffy white towel, which was fastened around the tops of her breasts and reached to midway down her thighs. 'How did you...?'

'Tea or coffee?' he again asked, looking up from the bottom of the stairs at her.

'How did you get in?' she demanded.

'Through the backdoor,' he replied nonchalantly, smiling as she hugged the towel tightly to her naked body. 'How do you think?'

'Get out of my house,' she said, without too much conviction.

'We'll have a cup of coffee and a little chat first, and then I'll go,' he said. 'You get yourself dressed and I'll make the drinks.'

Going into her room Emily sat on the end of her bed and felt dazed, determinedly keeping her eyes averted from the horrible pink implement lying so close by. Was there to be no reprieve from this torment? She should have left the chair jammed against the kitchen door. Arthur was in her house again. He was making coffee in the kitchen as if he lived there.

This really was the end, she thought miserably, slipping into a light summer dress, again not bothering with a bra. Brushing her damp hair back before leaving her bedroom, she crept into her parents' room and lifted the telephone receiver. Her only chance now, as she saw it, was Christine.

'I don't believe it,' she murmured, wondering why the phone didn't work. 'What's going on now? That's all I need.'

Going downstairs to find Arthur studying the photographs in the lounge, she folded her arms and scowled at him. 'You're a horrible man,' she said with passion, needing to get it off her chest.

'What are these?' he asked her, his expression thunderous. 'What are these photographs?'

'They're disgusting, that's what they are,' she said.

'You're telling me they are,' he agreed. 'Who took them? Have you had that yob Jack round here?'

'No, you know very well who took them,' she challenged. 'How dare you creep into my house, into my bedroom, when I'm sleeping?'

'I'm sorry?'

'You're a disgrace,' she hissed, her blood rising. 'You're vile and obscene. Get out of this house.'

'I really don't know what to say, Emily,' he said passively. 'Did that young scum take them?'

'You took them,' she accused, beginning to feel a little confused, beginning to doubt her own convictions. 'You crept round here with that disgusting vibrator thingy and you—'

'I've not been here since I left you to have your bath and get an early night,' he told her. 'Do you honestly think I'd creep into your room at night and play silly tricks on you?'

'Yes, I do.'

'And plant a vibrator on your bed and take photographs?' He shook his head. 'No, you're very much mistaken, young lady.'

Emily lifted her chin defiantly. 'Am I? Am I really?'

'Emily, I have more than enough evidence of your wickedness to see your father throw you out onto the streets,' he said casually. 'I don't have to set you up. I don't have to sneak in here at night with a camera and a vibrator. You've been caught red-handed, and there are no lies in the world that will get you out of this

65

one. I know you masturbate, but I didn't think for one moment that you had a vibrator.'

'I... I haven't,' she stammered, aghast at the suggestion. 'It's not mine!'

'It's obvious that you didn't take these photographs, Emily,' he said, ignoring her protestation, 'so I think you'd better tell me who did.'

'*You* did,' she insisted. 'You know you did.'

'To blame me just because you've been caught is feeble, young lady. Who took them? Unless you tell me I'll ring your parents and have them get on the next flight home to sort this out.'

Brushing her damp hair back from her brow, Emily began to wonder whether someone else had somehow crept into the house and taken the photographs. No, it was Arthur, it had to be. But how? The latch was up on the front door, the chair was wedged in place in the kitchen, and the downstairs windows were all closed. But somehow he had got in. She was sure it *had* to be him.

'You're right about one thing, Emily,' Arthur said, interrupting her confused thoughts as he flicked through the images. 'These are disgusting. Look at the way you're posing, pretending to be asleep.'

'I was asleep,' she maintained. 'I'd never pose like that, and certainly not with a... with a vibrator.'

'Who took the photographs, Emily?' he quizzed.

'I don't know,' she wailed, frustrated. 'Well I mean I do know - it was you.'

Arthur shook his head. 'I left here last night as you well know,' he stated flatly. 'So the only possible explanation is that someone called round and you let them in to indulge in your sordid games.'

'But—'

'But what? It's a simple, indisputable fact. You let someone into the house.'

'Oh, I've had enough of this,' Emily stormed, and moving to the lounge window she flipped aside the nets and indicated the closed casements. She then went through to the dining room, Arthur following with an amused expression on his face, and did the same. All the windows were closed and secure, as she knew they would be. No one could have got into the house. Was she going mad? No, it must have been Arthur, but she had no idea how he'd managed it. Turning, she snatched the photographs from him.

'They're mine,' she said.

'I know that,' he replied. 'Trying to make out they're mine was silly, wasn't it?'

'I didn't mean—'

'I know what you meant, young lady,' he growled, dragging the armchair into the centre of the room. 'Bend over the back again, if you please.'

'I didn't mean that I took the photos.'

'I realise that. What you meant was they're your photos; they belong to you. That's right, isn't it?'

'No, I—'

'The chair, young lady,' he ordered again.

Standing behind the piece of furniture, Emily felt her buttocks clench and her

66

stomach churn as she tried to prepare herself for another spanking. At least Arthur hadn't brought his cane, if that was any compensation. She was already becoming brainwashed into accepting this treatment, she realised - a spanking being acceptable and preferable to a caning. What did any of it matter? It didn't matter. Nothing mattered any more, she thought, as he again ordered her to bend over the back of her father's favourite armchair.

Reluctantly bending forward from the waist and adopting the required position, she held the chair's arms and squeezed her eyes shut as Arthur folded her dress up over her hips and tensed her buttocks in readiness for the gruelling spanking...

The palm of his hand smacked across the rounded flesh of her panty-clad bottom with a loud slap, and he pinned her down with his free hand on her neck. 'You're a filthy, disgusting little tart,' he growled, again slapping the sensitive flesh of her stinging bottom. 'You're a slut, a whore, a slag, a common little strumpet. Never have I had the misfortune to known such a dirty, filthy, smutty trollop.'

Letting out a pitiful yelp with every stinging slap, Emily listened to his unjust tirade. Again and again his palm splatted against her tight white panties, the sounds of her wails, the spanks and his heavy breathing filling the room. With the pain permeating the fiery globes of her bottom she began to wonder whether she was a slut. Perhaps Arthur was right.

Could he see, she wondered as her embarrassment soared, the sweet swell of her sex lips held snugly inside her panties? This was degradation, humiliation and violation beyond belief. But she was trapped by the man, she reflected.

'No cooling cream this time,' Arthur eventually said, halting the merciless spanking, his breathing strained. 'No special treatment for you like before. Now put your hands behind your back.'

'My hands behind my back?' she gasped from her bent position. 'What are you going to do to me now?'

'Bind your wrists,' he replied frankly, taking a short white piece of rope from a trouser pocket.

'Arthur, no please,' she begged as he crossed her arms on the small of her back and tied her wrists together.

'I have to do this, young lady,' he decreed. 'It's for your own good. With your wrists bound you can't touch yourself in wicked ways, or use your disgusting carnal toy.'

'May I stand up now, please?' Emily sulked, sniffing back a sob.

'Mr Price.'

'May I stand up now, please, Mr Price?'

'Yes, you may,' he allowed. 'Now, I've been pondering your attitude,' he continued once she'd stiffly straightened up and turned to face him, her eyes sparkling with unshed tears and her cheeks flushed, 'and it continues to disappoint me.'

As he turned to look out of the window Emily tried to free her wrists, but the rope was too well tied and too tight. She gazed wistfully at the photograph of her parents on the mantelpiece. Her mother was smiling, her father's expression stern. From the photograph they'd witnessed the spanking of their daughter's bottom, she mused ruefully.

Emily knew that she had to resign herself to the fact that she was now completely under Arthur's control. He'd wanted to play a major role in her life, and that's exactly what he'd achieved. But hopefully, once her parents were home, his unfair regime would at last come to an end.

She wondered what to do. The phone was out of order, and even if she managed to get out of the house, even if she could manage to avoid the beady surveillance of her odious neighbour, she could hardly walk down the street with her hands tied behind her back. Feeling utterly trapped she sat on the sofa and winced and squirmed a little as her stinging buttocks made contact with it.

'Arthur, you can't keep doing this to me,' she tried reasoning with him.

'Be quiet,' he said dismissively, turning back to look down at her. 'For now you'll only speak when spoken to. Do you understand me?'

Emily's shoulders sagged despondently. 'Yes, Mr Price,' she whispered, knowing any other response was pointless.

'Things have gone from bad to worse, Emily,' he said. 'If your parents knew you had that disgusting phallic *thing* upstairs they'd be destroyed.'

'But it isn't *mine*—'

'You will only speak when spoken to,' he silenced her angrily. 'If I have to tell you again you'll be in serious trouble. As it is you're in enough trouble already. The report book is evidence of that. I have an accurate catalogue of your disgusting behaviour. Never before have I had the misfortune to come across such a wanton, undisciplined young lady.'

Sitting on the sofa and hanging her head as Arthur ranted, Emily wondered where all this would end.

'I'll be back soon,' his diatribe finally drew to a close. 'And when I return I want to find you in a more compliant mood.'

Again struggling in vain to free her hands as she listened to him leave, she flopped back on the sofa and sighed resignedly. Gazing again at the photograph of her parents looking judgementally down upon her, she felt her shame and apprehension rising. She was in the family lounge with her hands tied behind her back, wearing a dress with no bra and her bottom pulsing from a recent spanking. They could never learn of the events overtaking her since they'd been away, she decided. Whatever it took, whatever she had to do, she'd make sure her parents never, ever knew anything of this. Even though she was sure they'd ultimately support her, she knew it would damage their faith in their daughter, and damage their friendship with their neighbour too, and she didn't want to be the cause of any fallings out - no matter how much she now loathed him.

Chapter 9

Having waited uneasily on the sofa for an hour, Emily jumped as she heard the backdoor open. Turning and looking at the lounge door she wondered what to expect now. Trembling, she waited in trepidation as she heard someone enter the kitchen and the backdoor close.

Arthur strolled into the lounge and gazed down at her struggling to sit up straight, not an easy task with her hands tied behind her back.

'I've been meaning to ask you something,' he said forthrightly. 'How many men have you made love with?'

The intrusive question came right out of the blue and Emily stared at him, utterly shocked by it and his audacity in asking it. 'How dare you ask such a thing?' she gasped.

'Oh come on, Emily,' he said, waving her objection away dismissively. 'How many?'

'Not that it's any of your business,' she stated curtly, looking up at him as he moved to stand before her, 'but I'm a virgin, if you must know.'

'A virgin?' he echoed, reaching out to stroke her hair. 'Really? At your age?'

'It's true,' she insisted, warily sensing a change of mood in the man. He seemed more like his old self. He seemed more approachable, more like the friendly neighbour she'd always known. 'I've never... I've never made love with anyone.'

'That's interesting...' Arthur mused. 'Very interesting, but a little difficult to believe, what with the way you've been behaving over the past few days.'

'Honestly, Arthur,' Emily insisted, wanting him to believe her now her secret was out, 'I am a virgin. I've never slept with anyone. Nobody's even touched me intimately.'

Arthur sat on the sofa beside her, his thigh resting against hers. 'Okay, Emily,' he comforted, patting her knee reassuringly, 'if you say so then I do believe you.' He smiled at her and she smiled at him, relieved. 'Now, I'll untie your hands for you.'

'Yes please, Arthur,' she sighed eagerly, 'I'd like you to do that.'

She turned her back a little and Arthur loosened the rope, pausing for a brief second to surreptitiously study her; her beautiful profile; her silky hair; her slender throat; the profile of her breast, and down to her thighs. He then slipped the rope into his trouser pocket and unaware of the brief inspection she'd just suffered, she turned back to face him, rubbing her wrists to get the circulation back.

'Is that better?' he asked.

'Yes, thank you,' Emily replied, her pulse quickening a little as she thought he looked fleetingly at her breasts, 'that's much better. I was getting pins and needles in my arms and my wrists were getting a little sore.'

'Yes, I'm sorry, but I had to teach you a lesson, you see?' he explained. 'Although perhaps I have been a little overzealous in my duties. I'm one of the old school, you see? And I've never before had to cope with a modern-day teenager.'

'No, I understand,' she conceded generously, smiling prettily at him.

'Thanks for being so understanding, Emily,' he said, putting his hand on her knee. 'I'm afraid I've made a bit of a hash of things,' he said apologetically, 'haven't I?'

'Oh no, Arthur,' she hastily tried to reassure him, putting a dainty hand on top of his where it rested on her knee. 'It's been all my fault, really. I should have been better behaved for you.'

He smiled and moved his hand just a fraction higher up her thigh. 'Thank you, my dear girl,' he said, 'you're such a sweet thing. I've always been extremely fond of you, and I'd hate to think we might fall out over all this.'

'We won't, Arthur,' she said with conviction, squeezing his hand as his hand squeezed her thigh. 'Really we won't.'

'That means a lot to me,' he said, and eased his hand down between her thighs just a little, despite her smooth limbs remaining tightly together. 'You really are a beautiful girl, Emily,' he went on, his eyes moving down and focussing on the tiny triangle of white peeping from between her thighs, just beneath the hem of her dress, his words and gaze making her somewhat uncomfortable.

'Arthur!' she admonished, playfully pushing against his shoulder, trying to lighten the suddenly intense atmosphere between them. There was a long moment's pause as he raised his eyes and scrutinised her clear face, pinning her with his stare. Emily held her breath, unsure of herself, and then he laughed and, greatly relieved, she exhaled and laughed too, all tension suddenly evaporating.

'I'm glad we've made up, Emily,' he went on.

'I have tried to behave,' she said, feeling she needed to put her point now they were on sensible talking terms again. 'I've done everything you've told me to and I've tried to be as obedient as I can be. But many of your demands on me are too unreasonable,' she explained. 'I've tried my best to be good, but you've asked too much of me.'

'I have?' he said amiably.

Emily nodded. 'It's true, you have,' she said. 'I've not known if I'm coming or going, and some of the things you've done to me...'

'But you continually argue and disobey,' he reasoned. 'I was only doing what your parents asked as best I could. But you continually made my task harder than it should be, Emily, and it was extremely tiresome.'

'I'm sorry,' she apologised.

'But now you'll do as you're told?' he asked, but seeing her stiffen a little he added, 'Let's meet each other halfway, okay?'

'Okay,' she agreed.

'Excellent,' he said. 'I understand that you want to go out in the evenings and have some fun with your friends.'

'Well yes, I do,' she confirmed, barely noticing the hand press a little further between her thighs, and move a little nearer that small white triangle of cotton.

'There you are, then,' he smiled. 'I'm only trying to help you.'

Emily was a little confused. 'You mean, you'll allow me out at night even though my father has said I have to stay in?' Both her hands were now resting around his wrist, but when his hand again moved a fraction closer to her panties she did nothing to stop it; clearly it was an innocent movement and she didn't want to embarrass him by making an issue of it.

'Of course I will,' he said. 'Things are different between us now, Emily. 'You're an adult, and so you deserve to be treated like one. I'm not such an old fuddy-duddy as to stand in your way of having some fun with your friends. So if you really want to go to the wine bar—'

'Yes I do, I do,' she beamed eagerly.

'You'd like to meet young Jack?'

'Yes, I would.'

'Very well,' he said. 'If it means that much to you, I'm prepared to cover for you if you want to go out at night. Would you like me to help you?'

Emily's brow furrowed as she considered this, the fingers between her thighs gently stroking their smoothness without meeting any complaint or resistance. 'I don't like the idea of lying to my parents,' she said.

'We won't lie, dear girl,' he reassured her. 'We'll just be a little conservative with the truth, that's all. What your mother and father don't know won't hurt them, now will it?'

'No, I suppose it won't,' she agreed, the prospect of freedom an enticing one. 'Thanks, Arthur.'

'Are you feeling more relaxed about things?' he asked her.

'Yes, I think so,' she replied.

'You're doing very well, Emily,' he praised her, somewhat cryptically. 'You're a star pupil, in fact. So tell me, where will you go this evening? To the wine bar?'

'Yes, I will,' she admitted. 'Jack might be there.'

'I'm sure he will be there,' he said. 'I know I would be if I were his age and had the chance of a date with you.' Emily blushed at the compliment and didn't notice the fingers stroking ever closer to her white cotton panties. 'And no doubt he'll be very pleased to see you. I've planned my evening, too.'

'You have?' she asked.

'Yes, I'm going to destroy the photographs I took of you and wipe the backups I made. And I'll have to make some changes to the report book, too; always home by ten as instructed, excellent behaviour etcetera etcetera. Your parents will be so pleased with you.'

'But you've already told them I got home late,' she reminded him. 'You rang my father.'

'I'll say I was mistaken. I'll say I heard someone in the street and assumed it was you. I'll tell them you've been staying at home, studying. If we stick to the same story you'll be all right. Are you happy with that?'

Emily nodded, brightening up even more. 'Yes,' she smiled. 'Yes I am.'

'Good, then I think we're going to get along very well from now on. Just like we always used to.'

With Arthur so close and in this sort of kind mood she suddenly felt strangely safe and secure. And having his hand between her thighs was innocent enough, wasn't it? More paternal than anything questionable. He was just being affectionate toward her, like he always used to be.

'That's good...' Arthur said in a low voice, although Emily was unsure to what he was referring. 'You're enjoying this, aren't you?' he asked, his fingers gently stroking between her closed thighs.

'En-enjoying what?' she whispered, a dangerous, confusing excitement starting to twist her insides, and a damp warmth beginning to simmer inside her panties.

'Us two,' he elaborated, 'talking like this, like we used to, friends again. What did you think I meant?'

'Oh,' Emily sighed, relieved, flustered, 'yes I'm enjoying it... I mean no, I didn't think you meant anything,' she rambled on, not knowing what she was saying but feeling the need to keep talking, wanting to keep him in this good mood but keeping her thighs defensively closed around his hand.

'That's good,' he smiled. 'I don't want us falling out again. We've been friends for so long, and I wouldn't want you thinking badly of me.'

'No, me neither,' she whispered.

Arthur gently extricated his hand and patted her knee again. 'Good, I'm glad we had this little chat. So I'll tear out the incriminating pages from the report book and we'll start afresh, yes?'

Emily nodded eagerly.

'I'm sure your parents will believe me if I say something like I spilled coffee over those particular pages.'

Arthur was more like his old self and Emily relaxed some more, but why this sudden change of attitude? From chaining her to the radiator, locking her in her house, binding her wrists and spanking and beating her, he was now relaxing the extreme restrictions on her and allowing her to go out. Had he changed tack because he knew his draconian methods weren't working? Whatever his reason, Emily sensed that she still had to be a little careful. But there again, he seemed his old sincere self, so perhaps she could now relax and enjoy the rest of her time alone at home until her parents got back from holiday.

'To put your father's mind at rest, and your mother's, I'll ring them this evening and report that you've been a model daughter,' Arthur continued, his hand squeezing her knee reassuringly.

'Ah yes, that reminds me,' Emily said, 'our phone doesn't work for some reason.'

'Oh?' Arthur looked surprised. 'I'll report the fault for you. I'm sure they'll get it back on soon. By the way,' he winked at her conspiratorially, 'you'd better hide your vibrator thing. You don't want your parents discovering it.'

'It really isn't mine,' Emily assured him. 'I've no idea where it came from.'

'Whatever you say,' he chuckled, as though he didn't believe her but pretended he did to save her embarrassment. 'But make sure you hide it well anyway.'

'I'll do better than that, I'll get rid of the obscene thing altogether,' she vowed. 'I certainly don't want it.'

'And the photographs you have?'

'Yes, yes I'll get rid of them too. I'll burn them.'

'Good girl,' he said, nodding thoughtfully. 'We don't want your parents discovering anything about this fortnight you wouldn't want them to, do we?'

'No we don't, thanks,' Emily agreed. This was all beginning to work out rather well, she thought, her spirits rising as she relaxed and the tension left her. Allowed out in the evenings with no definite curfew, the incriminating evidence destroyed; she had nothing to worry about now - apart from making sure she kept Arthur onside from hereon in. Perhaps he wasn't so bad after all, she reflected. Perhaps he really had only been trying to do what was best for her. She lifted one foot up onto the sofa, holding her ankle with both hands, her breasts moulding to her raised thigh, her chin resting on her knee. 'Sorry if I've been a bit of a pain, Arthur,' she said. 'I didn't mean to be.'

He smiled and shook his head. 'Let's say no more about it, eh?' he said, fleetingly eyeing the panties that were clearly visible to him now, the gentle swell of white cotton snugly cocooning her hidden sex.

Emily smiled and chatted to him as if oblivious to her exhibitionism, her chin remaining on her knee. She thought he could probably see her panties, but there was no harm in that, was there? This was Arthur, old friend of the family. Her parents would be happy to think he was giving up his time to take such an interest in her and make sure she was okay. 'I like you when you're like this,' she whispered sincerely, her moist lips slightly parted, her eyes wide and bright. 'It's like you always used to be with me. It's like we're friends again.'

'We are friends again,' he assured her, reaching out and stroking a few wisps of silky hair behind her dainty ear, his other hand boldly stroking right up her thigh until his fingers actually touched the front of her panties. It pressed there for long, long seconds, the silence hanging heavy between them, their eyes locked together, his searching hers, Emily suddenly aware of the ticking clock on the mantelpiece and the strange excitement churning in the pit of her stomach and the alien pressure against her sex lips...

And then as quickly as the hand had advanced it retreated and Arthur stood, a little stiffly, Emily thought.

'So you're okay?' he asked, his voice a little hoarse all of a sudden.

'Yes, I'm fine,' Emily replied, wondering why he asked but feeling happy thinking about getting ready for her evening out. She couldn't believe how things had changed. With no curfew to worry about she could go to the wine bar and then on to a nightclub and really enjoy herself. Life was looking good again, she reflected, feeling at ease for the first time since her parents had gone away. And it was going to get even better.

'I'll see you later,' Arthur said, moving to the lounge door, where he paused and gave her a lingering look.

'Okay,' Emily beamed happily, standing up too.

'I'll get to work on the report book,' he told her. 'You have a good time this evening.'

Emily nodded enthusiastically. 'Yes, yes I will,' she said. 'And thank you, Arthur.'

Chapter 10

Emily extricated the photographs from beneath the sofa. She'd burn them later, she decided, taking them up to her room. Gazing at the vibrator lying on her bed, she wondered again where it had come from. Then secreting the photographs and vibrator in her dressing table drawer, she sat on the end of her bed and gazed at her reflection in the mirror, wondering about those secret, pleasurable sensations she'd experienced when Arthur touched her. Of course he was only being friendly, it meant nothing to him, but they were hugely significant moments for her.

And there was something else - something she never would have believed only a short time before. There was something exciting too about knowing her next-door neighbour could see her panties. Lifting her foot onto the sofa, knowing the movement had raised the hem of her dress even higher, knowing it was wicked of her, was an impulsive but intentional tease, just to see how the man might react. And uncharacteristic though the move was it made her feel good - made her feel sexy. After years of being a beautiful but shrinking violet, she got an immense thrill from doing something so daring, so against the grain. It was not the sort of thing she'd normally consider doing, but in return for her freedom it was well worth it. Keeping Arthur happy would pay off, she thought, slipping out of her dress and putting on a fresh white bra and panties, then taking her miniskirt from the chair. The chances of her going on holiday to Tenerife were looking good again, and she was going to enjoy the rest of her time living alone. Nothing could go wrong now, she felt sure, as she fastened her skirt at her trim waist and slipped into a white blouse. Nothing could go wrong now... could it?

Applying her make-up and brushing her auburn hair, she reckoned Arthur wouldn't bother to wait up for her. Without the ten o'clock deadline to worry about he'd probably go to bed. With the phone out of order she decided to call at Christine's house on her way to the wine bar. Christine would be up for a night out, she thought happily as she glossed her succulent lips. Christine was usually up for anything.

Deciding she looked good, she skipped happily down the stairs. This was what these two weeks should have been like from day one, she mused, grabbing her small shoulder bag, stepping outside and pulling the front door closed.

'Emily,' Arthur called from his porch.

'Hi,' she trilled brightly. 'I'm just going to call for Chrissie and then we're off to the wine bar.'

'No, come round here,' he said. 'There's a bit of a problem.'

'A problem?' she echoed, suddenly panicking a little that something might have

74

happened to her parents.

'Your father just rang me,' he told her as she hurried up his garden path, his eyes flitting to her breasts and then back up to her face. 'He couldn't get through to you because your phone's still out of order.'

'Are they all right?' she asked anxiously. 'Nothing's happened, has it?'

'No, no they're both fine,' he reassured her. 'But the thing is, well, come into the house and I'll tell you.'

'What is it?' she asked, concern etched on her lovely face as he closed the front door and ushered her into his lounge.

'They were about to go on some coach excursion to one of those organised barbecues,' he started to explain. 'That's why there wasn't time for me to come and get you.'

'Yes?' Emily urged. 'So what's the matter?'

'The thing is,' he said, 'your father's going to ring back later to talk to you. He and your mother just want to know how you are. It's quite understandable.'

'Oh,' she sighed with relief, 'is that all? That's all right, isn't it? Good grief, I thought it was something serious for a minute.'

'Yes, but it means you'll have to be here when he rings,' he pointed out.

'Oh, of course, yes I see,' Emily sighed despondently, seeing her evening out disappearing before her eyes.

'Bearing in mind he doesn't want you going out in the evenings at all this is very inconvenient for you,' he went on, explaining what Emily had already realised.

'What time is he going to ring?' she asked.

'That's the trouble, I don't know,' he told her. 'We were cut off before he could say. Presumably when they get back from their evening out, which could be at any time. I really am sorry about this, Emily,' he sighed, shaking his head with apparent regret. 'Of all the rotten luck, just when you were looking forward to going out so much.'

'Ah well, it's a shame but it can't be helped, I suppose,' she sighed bravely, sitting on the sofa. 'There's always tomorrow night.'

'But you must have been so looking forward to going out this evening,' said Arthur.

'Yes I was, but if he phones early enough I'll still be able to make it to the wine bar,' she said, brightening again.

'Yes, that's true,' he agreed, going into the kitchen and returning with a bottle of wine and a couple of glasses. 'I must say, you look lovely this evening, Emily. Very attractive indeed.'

'Oh, thank you,' she said, blushing prettily and fidgeting a little where she sat on the sofa.

'Yes, very attractive...' he mused, his eyes moving over her. 'Would you like a glass of wine?' he asked, holding the bottle up for her to see.

'Yes please,' she replied, smiling at him. 'I might as well while I'm waiting.'

'Don't you go telling your father,' he laughed, placing the glasses on the sideboard and taking a corkscrew from one of the drawers, with which he opened the wine.

'I won't if you don't,' Emily giggled.

'That's my girl,' he chuckled, passing her a glass of white, fragrant wine.

Although disappointed about her evening out, Emily felt quite at ease sitting in Arthur's lounge. It was as if he'd returned to his old self, the friendly neighbour she'd looked upon as a kind uncle.

'The photographs,' she began, sipping her wine, 'have you destroyed them yet?'

'Yes I have,' he said reassuringly. 'You have nothing more to worry about.' He took a sip of his wine and then moved to sit beside her. 'Yes, you do look very attractive this evening.'

Emily shifted awkwardly again, uncomfortable receiving such overt praise. 'Thanks,' she said quietly, and sipped her own wine.

'And I like your blouse, and your skirt... although it is a little short.'

Emily blushed even deeper and tried to smooth the hem down her thighs a little, but failed. 'It isn't that short,' she said.

'Why do girls wear their skirts so short these days?' he asked conversationally, his gaze resting on her thighs, watching her hand struggle in vain to lower the hem.

'Because it's the fashion,' she said, before repeating, 'but mine isn't *that* short.'

'Why is it the fashion?'

'I don't know. It just is.'

'It's the fashion because girls want to show off their legs, Emily,' he told her. 'Girls wear make-up to look attractive to men, and girls show off their legs to attract men.'

'Well I don't,' she said.

'Don't you?' he mused. 'Are you sure about that?'

No, Emily wasn't sure about that, but she wasn't going to admit as much to Arthur.

'Are you sure you don't flirt so men will notice and admire you; admire your figure; your breasts; you bottom; your legs...'

'Arthur!' Emily gasped, shocked by his words. 'All I want is to dress fashionably, look pretty and be able to go out and enjoy myself with my friends.'

'I quite understand that,' he said, his tone placatory. 'I'm fully on your side, my dear. But the first thing we must do is ensure your parents know nothing about your secret life.'

'My secret life?' she giggled, the wine warming her blood pleasantly. 'You make it sound awful.'

'That's what you're leading by dressing like you are; a secret life,' he said conspiratorially. 'Don't get me wrong, I think you look very nice, but I'm pretty sure your parents wouldn't be so understanding. We'll have to work together to make sure you can continue to enjoy yourself once they return from holiday.'

'I don't want to lie to them, Arthur,' she said warily.

'So we'll have to be clever to make sure they never find out, hm?'

Emily took another sip of the delicious wine, her head feeling nicely light, her spirits increasingly carefree 'Nice?' she chirped, giving his arm a playful slap.

'Pardon?' Arthur said, almost spilling a little wine.

'Nice,' she repeated with a mischievous pout. 'You said I only look *nice*.'

'Aha, I wondered if you'd notice that,' he laughed, and Emily laughed with him, and then his expression grew serious and he added, 'To say any more might be inappropriate, Emily...'

That heavy, uncomfortable silence settled over them again as they stared at each other, and then Emily inhaled deeply and sipped her wine, the hand holding her glass trembling slightly, Arthur's eyes flickering to where her blouse stretched over her breasts as she nervously filled her lungs.

'Well, I...' she started, having swallowed quite a large mouthful of the golden liquid.

'Do you like it?' he asked. 'The wine, do you like it?'

'Yes, thank you,' she whispered. 'Why are you prepared to help me?' she asked, wanting to forget that awkward moment just passed and again pondering his dramatic change of attitude.

'Because, as I see it, I have no choice,' he said enigmatically.

Emily frowned and finished her drink. 'What do you mean?' she asked, barely aware of him taking the empty glass from her hand and refilling it.

'Well, rather than let you loose, possibly getting yourself into trouble, I can guide you, Emily,' he explained, setting his own glass aside on the occasional table, only half empty. 'I can point you in the right direction. I can be a great help to you. I'm not just some old fool who knows nothing, you know. I was young once, and I can give you the benefit of my experience.' His hand moved back to her thigh as it had that afternoon, and to Emily, with a glass-and-a-half of fine white wine inside her, combined with his reassuring words, it felt extremely comforting.

His fingers stroked for a few seconds as he watched her reaction closely, and then he went on. 'For example, if your parents find this skirt in your bedroom, they'll know immediately that something's going on.'

'That's true,' she whispered thoughtfully. 'I hadn't really thought that far ahead.'

'So what do we do about that little problem?' he asked, his hand moving in small circles that made her skin tingle nicely.

Emily frowned as she sipped more wine and pondered his question. 'Well, I'm... I'm not too sure,' she finally admitted.

'We hide your fashionable clothes round here,' he announced dramatically. 'In that way you can buy as much as you like, and I'll look after it for you without your parents ever knowing. Then whenever you go out on the pretext of going to study with Christine, you can slip round here, get changed, and then meet your friends in town.'

Emily beamed at him, her eyes sparkling with joy. 'That's brilliant!' she exclaimed. 'Would you really do that for me, Arthur?'

'Of course I would,' he said. 'We're friends, aren't we?'

'Yes!' she enthused. 'Yes we are!'

'Good. If it makes you happy, then I'm happy...'

His eyes dropped to her thighs again, to where his hand moved almost imperceptibly on her smooth flesh. Emily's eyes followed his, and together they sat in silence while he caressed her.

'Arthur...'

'Your skirt is very short, though,' he said, his voice suddenly low, even a little strained. 'That alone could get you into all sorts of trouble. It's a good job I'm here to look after you.'

'Arthur...'

'I can even glimpse a little of your panties, Emily,' he went on. 'Just imagine what might happen if I was a young lad with no self-control.'

His hand applied a little pressure and her thighs parted just a fraction. Emily tensed a little, resisting, curiously watching the hand pressing against her leg. Feeling a little unsure of herself, her embarrassment rising, she squeezed her thighs together again, trapping the hand between them.

'Don't worry, Emily,' he coaxed, 'I've seen it all before. I'm just helping you, remember? You'd be surprised just how many girls show off their knickers to us men. That's what miniskirts are all about. That's the name of the game, like a secret weapon, luring us.'

'Is that what you think?' she asked, feeling increasingly light-headed but enjoying the relaxing sensation and sipping some more wine. 'I'd never thought of it like that.'

'No, you wouldn't. You see, with all due respect, you're incredibly naïve. But that's where I can help you.'

Relaxing as she finished her second glass of wine, Emily allowed him to take it from her again, her thighs falling fractionally apart. Arthur poured a third glass and passed it to her as she slumped back a little on the sofa, a rosy hue prettily colouring her cheeks.

'For example, did you know I could see your panties this afternoon, when we were sitting together on your sofa?' Arthur asked.

Emily nodded. 'Yes, I did,' she admitted, 'but that's different.' She giggled, putting her free hand over her mouth. 'I mean, you're *Arthur.*'

'And that's my point,' he said. 'What if I wasn't good old Arthur? What if I was some lad with his hormones all over the place? What might have happened then, hm?'

Emily frowned, trying to fathom out his point.

'And do you know I can see your panties again now, Emily?' he said, and watched the girl as she took a tiny sip of wine and then nodded again. 'And you don't mind that?'

Emily thought for a few seconds. 'I don't know, really,' she said. 'I suppose you shouldn't be looking.'

'But you shouldn't be flaunting them at me, now should you?'

'No,' Emily acknowledged contritely, but a definite pressure from his hand indicated that she wasn't to move into a more modest position.

'No, you shouldn't,' he concurred. 'And shall I show you what might happen if you were to tease - intentionally or unintentionally - some randy youth who couldn't control his urges?'

Emily did not move or say anything. She just watched the man closely.

'Well, shall I?' he pressed.

'What are you going to do?'

'I want you to look upon this as education, Emily,' he told her. 'This is to help you, nothing more. Do you understand me? It's nothing more than that. At my age I get nothing from it. I'm simply doing this to help you. Okay?'

She said nothing, her uncertain silence the response he needed, so he slipped down from the sofa and knelt before her and placed his hands on her knees.

He was genuinely trying to help her, she was sure, as with his steady stare he silenced any uncertainties she may have voiced, then when happy she was going to remain silent, parted her thighs and gazed between them, directly at the triangular gusset of her white panties.

As she looked down at what he was looking at, she told herself that things were going to change for the better now that she and Arthur understood each other. With the benefit of his experience she'd be more worldly-wise and therefore more confident, and as he slowly pushed her thighs even further apart she knew she had him to thank for that.

He looked deep into her eyes, his fingers squeezing the smooth flesh of her parted thighs. She was totally open to him. She sat quietly and meekly, waiting to see what he did next, not knowing how best to react.

His eyes lowered, following the slim line of her throat, down to her cleavage, it's shadowy depths made visible by the open neck of her blouse.

'You have lovely breasts, Emily,' he suddenly said, shocking her with his frankness.

'Arthur, you shouldn't—'

'Any red-blooded youth will be drooling to get his hands on them,' he went on. 'I'm only warning you; with such loveliness you need to be careful.'

Watching, spellbound as Arthur pressed his fingers into the naked flesh of her inner thighs and then inched them nearer her crotch, Emily was sure she was safe with him. He genuinely seemed to be helping her. And with him on her side, her ally, she'd have no trouble getting out at night and enjoying her life for a change.

'W-what are you doing?' she asked, as Arthur's fingers finally reached the triangle of white cotton and rested against it.

'It's all right,' he crooned. 'Now just move your bottom forward a little, and I'll show you what I'm doing.'

'Are you sure...?' she whispered. 'Okay...' and she wriggled a little, sliding to the front edge of the sofa until he knelt between her knees, 'if you're sure...'

'You see here?' he breathed, pushing his hands up to her flat stomach and folding her skirt around her hips.

'No, what?' she whispered, watching his every move with endearing intensity.

'Here...' he said, and moved his hands back down between her thighs until his thumbs pressed and stroked her cotton-covered sex lips.

'Ooh,' she gasped, tensing slightly. 'Arthur, I don't think—'

'You see, they're damp, just here...' A finger centred and pressed a little more between her hidden sex lips, making her gasp again and her cheeks blush even more. She inhaled sharply and arched her back a little, just her shoulders supporting her against the back of the sofa, and he devoured the vision of her breasts pressing forward against her blouse, the outline of her awakening nipples clearly visible.

'Can you feel that, my dear?' he asked, and watched Emily nod, her eyes closing, her succulent lips parting; gorgeous, pouting lips just made for...

'How does it feel...?'

'I-I'm not sure,' she whispered. 'Nice, I think. But you shouldn't be—'

'I'm just demonstrating what trouble you could get into. How do you think a lad would react if he knew you were turned on and wetting your knickers like this?'

'I - I suppose he might try to fuck me,' she said, the frankness of the words sounding incredibly sexy coming from such innocent lips.

'He might,' he agreed. 'Or for starters he might do this...' and pausing a moment to make sure she was still under his spell, and the wine's spell, Arthur leaned closer, lower, pressed his face between her parted thighs and touched a light kiss to her panties, inhaling her sweet fragrance through flared nostrils.

'Oh Arthur...' she sighed, 'you should stop now. This isn't right...'

Arthur pulled back a little and watched the beautiful girl. Her eyes were still closed and she was mumbling soft words, her head resting back on the sofa. The wine glass was sloping precariously to one side in the loose grip of her delicate fingers, threatening to spill the last of its contents onto his sofa. He carefully prised it from her, not wanting to break the spell, and stood it quietly on the carpet.

'How did that feel, Emily?' he whispered, and there was a long silence while she tried to decipher how it felt.

'Naughty... it felt naughty,' she eventually whispered back. 'I think I should go home now and wait there...'

'But I've not finished the first part of your education yet,' he said. 'You do still want me to help you, don't you?'

Emily's little tongue appeared and licked her lower lip, and then she nodded.

'Good girl,' he drawled.

'But I'm confused,' she confessed in hushed tones, her eyes still closed, her head still resting back. 'I know I'm naïve, but this can't be right. We shouldn't be doing this.'

'Nonsense, my dear,' Arthur coaxed. 'Just trust me. I'm doing all this for you. You'll thank me, I promise you will.'

In Emily's drifting thoughts Arthur's voice sounded distant. She could feel his fingers and thumbs stroking her thighs and touching her sex lips through her panties, and it did feel nice. The idea was to keep him on her side, not to upset him by being silly. Wishing her father would hurry up and phone so she could have her chat with him and then go home, she couldn't help moving her hips a little closer to the edge of the sofa so those fingers could touch her a little more easily. She should go home, but she felt nice and relaxed. If only her father would hurry up and phone...

Arthur lowered his head and kissed the front of her panties again. It was the end of the day and his stubble rasped lightly against the pure softness of her thighs, which instinctively squeezed against his face on both sides. Emily moaned, breathing deeply, and moved her hands to his head, her fingers entwining in his greying hair.

He moved his hands and squeezed them beneath her thighs, cupping them and pulling her closer. He inched his hands higher, until they were sandwiched between his sofa and her exquisite buttocks. Emily's breathing quickened and she lifted her head from the back of the sofa, watching with misty eyes the man squatting between her parted thighs, his head moving as he kissed and suckled the front of her panties. It was all so surreal. She'd known this man for years. He was their next-door neighbour, a good friend of the family, and here he was massaging her bottom and pulling her crotch tight against his face, nuzzling against her intimacies like a hungry animal. The shame was terrible... the excitement wonderful. She knew it was hopelessly, horribly wrong, but she also knew her hands were urging his head tighter between her thighs, knew her hips were urging her sex against his lips and nose.

A delicious sensation grew in her stomach and her head lolled back again, her eyes closing once more. It was building, threatening to overwhelm her. This could not happen. This must not happen. Arthur was carrying her towards a climax with his mouth. She gasped and stiffened, feeling his tongue press against her panties, taking the soaking material a little way between her sex lips. This was shameful, and just as her orgasm was about to burst forth Emily pressed against his head. 'No,' she pleaded, 'you can't, please, stop now, this is wrong...'

'Emily, which way do you want it?' Arthur asked, panting a little, sitting back on his ankles.

Emily opened her eyes and looked quizzically at the man kneeling between her parted thighs. 'What do you mean?' she asked him, all too aware of the tight material of her panties so exposed and vulnerable before him. 'Which way do I want what?'

'I'm trying to help you, but I'm not sure you're accepting my help.'

'I do—'

'You're resisting me, Emily.

'No, I'm not.

'I'm prepared to go as far as covering up for you where your parents are concerned. They've been my good friends for many years now, but still I've agreed to cover for you. But it seems that whatever I try to do you resist me. It's got to be give and take, young lady. This isn't a one-way street, you know.'

'I do know that,' she whispered urgently. 'I'm not resisting you, honestly I'm not. It's just that I don't want you to... I've never... I'm embarrassed, Arthur, don't you understand that?'

'And I'm at a loss as to what more I can do to help you,' he countered. 'Don't *you* understand that?'

'Yes, but—'

'The choice is yours, Emily. Which way do you want it? Either you want my help or you don't. It makes no odds to me. You either stay in all the time, as your father instructed, or you go out at night and have some fun. I either cover for you or I don't. You think about it and decide while I refill your glass.'

He stood and picked up their two glasses, then went back out to the kitchen to open another bottle.

Arthur had been a good friend over the years, but what, Emily wondered, was he thinking? What *did* he want, exactly? He was thinking something, planning something, but what was it? What thoughts lurked in his male mind? Was he sulking? Was he disappointed in her? He wanted to continue being her friend, that's all. As he said, he wanted to help her. Was it as simple as that? Would it be best to stop being childish and let him give her the benefit of his experience?

He returned, looking stern, and gave her a fresh glass of wine. He then sat in his armchair and stared at her as she sipped it, eyeing her shapely calves, her thighs - significantly together again - her trim waist, her breasts, her inviting cleavage. Remaining silent as he scrutinised her, he sipped his fresh glass of wine too.

'I wonder when my father will phone,' Emily said, wanting to break the uncomfortable silence enshrouding the room.

'I don't know,' he murmured dismissively. 'You might as well go home and wait there. There's no point in sitting here all evening. I'll come and get you when he does.'

'Oh, all right,' she said, finishing her drink and standing up, swaying a little from the alcohol, feeling bad, like she'd let Arthur down. 'I might see you later, then?'

'I'll come and get you when he phones,' he said bluntly.

Returning to her house on decidedly shaky legs, Emily sat on the sofa and shook her befuddled head. Once again she was totally confused. She wanted to get on with Arthur, wanted to accept his help, but he was making it impossible. No, *she* was making it impossible. He was right; whatever he'd tried to do to help her, she'd resisted him. She was behaving like a spoilt brat. He was only trying to help, she reflected, reclining on the sofa, her head spinning when she closed her eyes. He was only trying to help.

Chapter 11

Waking on the sofa the following morning, Emily looked around the lounge and rubbed her bleary eyes. The wine had made her sleep heavily. Feeling a little groggy she hauled her aching body up from the sofa and stretched her arms. What would today bring? What else lay in store for her?

Going through to the kitchen and filling the kettle, she couldn't think why her father hadn't phoned. Perhaps he had but Arthur thought it too late to disturb her. Again wishing her phone wasn't out of order she spooned some instant coffee into a mug and looked out of the window. It was a warm day, but raining steadily.

After a bowl of cereal Emily took a shower and put on a summer dress. Gazing in the mirror and admiring the way the dress accentuated her feminine curves, she wondered what Arthur was doing - and for some strange reason, what he'd think of her in this dress. Vague, blurred memories of something that had happened between the two of them the night before meandered in and out of her head...

Dismissing the silly images, putting them down to being so unused to drinking wine, she reflected that it would be nice to have a quiet day, deciding to do a little housework. No Arthur, no problems; although she very much doubted she'd be left alone for very long.

Noticing the pink vibrator as she was about to close her dressing table drawer, she felt her stomach somersault. Should she try it? Clutching the rude device she examined the smooth shaft and the rounded tip, the lure of it overwhelming, the temptation too much to resist. Feeling tense and a little hung-over she was in need of the relaxing relief of an orgasm.

Closing her bedroom door, she slipped her panties off and lay on her bed. Blushing as she parted her legs, she pulled her dress up over her stomach and gazed down at the gentle rise of her sex mound. Stroking her soft pubic curls and caressing her sex lips she felt a quiver run up her spine. She was becoming wet and held her breath as delicious sensations simmered, unable to suppress a little moan of pleasure.

This was wrong, she thought, imagining her father discovering her as he apparently had before. How was she ever going to face him again?

But desperate to appease her increasing desires such thoughts drifted from her head, and she switched the vibrator on and slipped the buzzing tip between the wet lips of her vagina. What if Arthur heard her, if he had his ear pressed to the other side of her bedroom wall? The last thing she wanted was to get in the bad books of her next-door neighbour again.

Her clitoris responding to the heavenly vibrations, the sensitive protrusion sending ripples of pleasure through her contracting womb, she closed her eyes and relaxed. 'Mmm... God,' she breathed as her clitoris pulsated beneath the buzzing tip of the vibrator. Her juices of arousal flowing freely, seeping down between the rounded cheeks of her bottom, she arched her back and gasped as she neared her climax. Never had she known such amazing sensations. Massaging her clitoris to orgasm with her fingers had been nothing like this. Her young body trembling uncontrollably, her eyes closed, she rolled her head from side to side and cried out as she finally exploded into a blissful orgasm.

Secretly thrilled that she hadn't disposed of the vibrator as she had previously vowed to, Emily shuddered as her orgasm ebbed. Her thighs tensed, her stomach hollowed, her breasts rose as she arched her back, and she again cried out as her young body quivered for long moments and then gradually went limp on the bed, doing her best to stifle her final sighs of delight.

She'd keep the vibrator, she decided dreamily as a final, gentle wave of pleasure washed over her. She'd hide it somewhere. She'd found a secret lover, a secret friend, and she wasn't about to give him up now, although when her parents were back she'd have to wait until they'd gone out before allowing her secret lover to appease her yearnings.

Switching the vibrator off as she thought she heard Arthur calling her, she propped her languid body up on her elbows. He wasn't in the house, was he? She should have known he'd not allow her any privacy, but she'd thought things had changed back to the way they always had been between them.

'Are you there, Emily?' he called.

'Damn!' she breathed, slipping the wet shaft beneath her pillow, hastily getting off her bed and just managing to slip her panties back on before she heard his footfall at the top of the stairs.

'Ah, there you are,' he said, opening the door and walking into her room. He was wearing a light raincoat, the shoulders of it a little wet. 'Are you ready?'

'Ready?' she frowned, turning away and trying to conceal her flushed complexion, her heart hammering in her chest.

'Are you ready to continue with your education?'

'Education...?' Awful images flickered into her head, but were gone again almost instantly. All she could really remember was up to the point where Arthur was sitting beside her on his sofa. Any other vague memories of what happened after that were too ridiculously awful to have actually taken place. She must have been dreaming really deeply during the night.

'Last night I asked you which way you wanted it,' he reminded her. 'So have you made your mind up?'

'I don't want anything any way,' she returned, brushing her auburn fringe away from her flushed brow as she gazed out of the window and tried to remember more of the previous evening. 'And I don't think you should barge into my bedroom like this.'

'I'm playing an active role in your life, Emily,' he stated matter-of-factly. 'If I need to come up to your bedroom to speak to you, then I will.'

'Surely I'm allowed some privacy?'

'Emily, time is running out,' he said, getting back to the point. 'Your parents will be home before we know it. So I'll ask you again: which way do you want it?'

'Which way do I want what?'

Arthur sighed, somewhat impatiently. 'Do you want to enjoy more freedom?' he asked. 'Do you want me to cover for you where your parents are concerned?'

'Yes,' she hastily confirmed. 'I mean... Arthur, I really don't know what I want.'

'Well as I said last night: if you want me to be your friend, your ally, then I'm here. And if you want to learn from my experience in life, well then again, I'm here.'

'I just want to be normal,' she said sadly, rubbing her temples, the excessive wine consumed during the previous evening still making her feel less than great. 'That's all I want, Arthur.'

'And I can help you in that,' he said. 'So it's up to you...'

Up to her third glass of wine Emily could remember what they'd discussed the previous evening. 'Nothing's changed,' she said warily, unsure of what had been said after that point. 'I still want your help, Arthur. I still want you to help educate me.' She couldn't remember much, if anything, about the education bit, but it sounded like something she needed.

'Very well, that's good.' He smiled and nodded with satisfaction. 'Now let's go round to my house and have a nice cup of coffee, shall we?'

'Did my father ring last night?' she asked, following him down the stairs to the front door.

'No,' he informed her. 'It must have been too late by the time they got back from their evening out.'

Emily reached to take her light, waterproof jacket from the coat stand, but Arthur stopped her. 'No,' he said, 'there's no need for that. If we hurry you'll not get wet...'

'You'll not get wet,' Emily grumbled to herself as she ran round to his front door, just as a particularly heavy deluge swept down from the grey rain clouds. 'Yeah, right.' She stood hunched under his porch and turned to watch him sauntering up the path, the collar of his raincoat turned up against the sudden squall. Despite only being out in the open for the few seconds it took her to run down her front path, the few yards along the pavement and then up Arthur's front path, her dress was soaked through and clung wetly to every curve of her shapely body. Her hair was wet, and strands clung to her cheeks and her fringe was stuck to her forehead.

'Ooohhhh, I'm cold,' she complained, rubbing her bear arms as he unlocked his front door and ushered her inside and along the hall into his kitchen.

'Cold?' he queried, filling the kettle. 'But it's a warm day, despite the rain.'

'It might be,' she moaned, 'but I'm wet and therefore I'm cold. It's all right for you,' she added, nodding at his raincoat as he took it off and hung it on the peg on his backdoor, 'you had that on.'

'True, I did,' he chuckled, eyeing her wet dress as he took two mugs down from a wall unit, the delicate material clinging to her, moulding to her firm breasts, her flat tummy, her youthful hips and her toned thighs. It was virtually transparent, her underwear just teasingly visible through the drenched material. 'You'd better get out of that,' he advised, indicating the garment, watching her shiver a little.

'Take it off?' she gasped. 'I can't do—'

'You'll catch your death if you don't,' he said across her. 'Come on, don't be silly, I've seen you in your underwear before.'

'Yes,' she said, 'but that's when I was younger. That was different. It didn't matter then.'

'Take it off, Emily,' he said firmly. 'I don't want your mother coming home and finding you ill with a cold or the flu. I don't want her accusing me of not looking after you properly.'

'Well have you got something else I can put on instead?' she asked.

He chuckled. 'And do I look like a man who'd have a wardrobe of women's clothing just hanging in his bedroom?' he asked.

Emily blushed prettily, knowing it was futile to argue, and unbuttoning the front of her dress she slipped it off and stood uncomfortably, holding the sodden material in one hand, uncertain what to do with it. Arthur gazed at her, her tight white bra holding her breasts snugly, faint round shadows indicating the outline of her nipples, and down to her tiny white panties, another faint, triangular shadow evidence of her pubic hair.

She squeezed her legs together in a vain attempt to conceal her slightly damp underwear, and her free hand lifted protectively towards her breasts, hovered awkwardly, and then lowered again. Arthur nodded agreeably and smiled as he focused on the ripe, smooth flesh filling her straining bra, her cleavage deep and shadowy.

'I don't know why you're so shy,' he said. 'Relax, I'm not going to bite.'

'I'm embarrassed,' she replied honestly. 'Any girl would be embarrassed standing in her underwear before her next-door neighbour.'

'But why be embarrassed?' he quizzed. 'We've known each other for years.'

'It makes no difference how long we've known each other. I'm an eighteen-year-old girl, a young woman, and I find it embarrassing standing here like this in front of you.'

'But I'm not just a neighbour, Emily, am I?' he said. 'We've always got on so well together. We're good friends, aren't we?'

'But I wouldn't stand like this in front of my parents, let alone a male friend.'

'Perhaps we're more than friends,' he suggested, focusing meaningfully on her bra again.

'What do you mean by that?'

'Just what I said,' he stated simply. 'Perhaps we have something other than just a friendship. Perhaps the time has come to...

'Are you still cold?' he suddenly asked, lifting his eyes again to her lovely face.

'No, I'm quite warm now.'

'But you're shivering.'

'A little, yes,' she acknowledged as he poured her a coffee and moved close to hand it to her.

'Here, get that inside you,' he said, remaining close in front of her. 'Then that will become a part of your ongoing education, Emily,' he went on.

'What will?' she asked.

'Fighting your embarrassment,' he qualified. 'You shouldn't be embarrassed about your body. You should be proud of it. You should be pleased that I enjoy looking at you. You have a lovely body, my dear... a really lovely body.'

'Arthur...' she whispered awkwardly, looking into his face, trying to decipher his thoughts, 'you shouldn't be saying that.'

He moved and Emily stiffened. He touched her hand, his fingers lingering on it for long seconds as he held her eyes with his, and then he took the wet dress from it and draped it over one of the kitchen chairs.

'You must learn to deal with your embarrassment, my dear,' he said, his voice a monotone. 'Sit down,' he went on, pulling another chair out from beneath the table for her, then doing the same for himself and sitting facing her.

'Thank you,' she said shyly.

Sipping his steaming coffee he smiled at her. 'You see, it's working already.'

'What is?' she asked.

'You're looking more relaxed already,' he said.

'I don't feel it,' she admitted. 'I feel uncomfortable in my underwear with you so close, with you looking at me.'

'But as I said, Emily, you have a lovely body and you should be proud of it. You have firm, shapely breasts.'

'Arthur, don't.'

'A very inviting cleavage.'

'Inviting?' she gasped, shocked. 'In what way inviting?'

His eyes moved lower. 'A flat stomach.'

'You really shouldn't.'

'Trim hips.'

'Arthur, I...'

His eyes continued their downward journey. 'Toned, slender thighs.'

'I think I'd better be going.'

'Smooth, healthy skin,' he concluded, and looked back up at her face, staring deeply into her wide, clear eyes. 'You certainly have no reason to be embarrassed about anything. And particularly not with me. I'm your friend. I'm on your side, remember?'

'My side?'

'Against your parents.'

'Arthur, I don't like the idea of going against my parents,' she stated. 'I don't want to lie to them. I don't like the idea of that.'

Arthur tutted and shook his head. 'And neither do I, Emily,' he told her. 'I don't believe in lying, you should know that. We'll just be doing a little covering up for you. And I'll be doing the covering, so you don't have to worry your pretty little head about that.' He lifted a finger and tapped the tip of her nose affectionately.

'How are you going to do that?' she asked, concern reflecting in her eyes.

'Well, for example,' he started pensively, 'if you say to me that you want to go out for an evening, I'll ask your parents whether they'd mind if I take you out somewhere. They'd have no problem with that if they thought we were going somewhere worthwhile; a play to help with your studies, something like that. I'll drop you in town, and then while you're enjoying yourself with your friends I will go to the theatre or the cinema. I generally go by myself anyway, so I won't mind that. Then I'll pick you up afterwards, bring you home, and no one will be any the wiser.'

Emily smiled gratefully, but looked uncertain. 'I still feel bad about it,' she admitted.

'Perhaps you'd rather stay at home during the evenings and study, instead of being out having fun with your friends?' he said, squeezing her knee encouragingly.

'I don't know what I want,' she replied, glancing down at the hand on her leg. 'It just doesn't seem right.'

'What doesn't?'

'Any of it,' she answered. 'Any of this.'

'Why not?'

'Well, I shouldn't be sitting here with you, like this, in just my bra and panties.'

'It's all about boosting your confidence, Emily.'

'My confidence doesn't need boosting,' she said, but she realised that his attention and compliments were making her feel a little less shy already, and the more she thought about Arthur helping her, the more she thought it just might work. Yes, it was the right way to go, she decided, relaxing just a little. Arthur looked at her, focused on the tiny white triangle of cotton tapering down between her thighs, and gave her a reassuring smile. He was an older man with greying hair; she was safe in his hands.

'Time is running out,' he reminded her. 'When your parents get back things will have to revert to the way they were - on the face of it, at least. Unfortunately we've wasted valuable time already, but now we understand each other we should be able to make some progress. Unless you trust me, however, unless you put yourself in my hands completely, we'll get nowhere. You either comply absolutely, or we forget it.'

'Comply?' she asked.

'Yes, give yourself completely to my experience and methods,' he qualified. 'Work hard with me and we might just have enough time for me to help you before your parents return.'

Emily thought about what he was saying for a few moments. 'Very well,' she eventually said, somewhat carefully.

'That's my girl,' he said, smiling, and then they sat together in silence for a while, sipping their coffee, looking at each other over the rims of their mugs as they drank.

'I'm sorry,' Emily said softly, placing her empty mug back on the kitchen table.

'Sorry?'

'I shouldn't have behaved so childishly with you before. It's made your job of looking out for me more difficult than it should be. I should be grateful to you, not making your life difficult.'

'Don't apologise,' he smiled, squeezing her knee warmly, his hand inching up her thigh a little. 'If anyone should apologise it's me.'

'You?' she queried. 'Why?'

'Because I came down too hard on you, Emily,' he said. 'I was trying to please your parents when I should have been considering you more all along.'

'So this is a fresh start,' she smiled.

'It is,' he concurred, nodding, making no disguise of eyeing the upper slopes of her breasts swelling enticingly from the cups of her bra, then his eyes crawled down to the white cotton between her thighs, then completely out of the blue his hand caressed along her thigh and he actually pressed his fingers against her there.

They sat in silence, staring at each other, neither of them moving, his fingers wedged between her thighs, pressing against the front of her panties.

'Is that nice?' he eventually asked.

'I... I thought,' she stammered, as he began to massage the soft swell of her sex lips through her flimsy panties.

'Yes, what did you think?' he coaxed.

'I didn't think this was a sexual thing,' she whispered.

'It's not a sexual thing, Emily,' he countered gently.

'Then why are you...' she didn't want to hurt the man's feelings by implying something improper, buy making inaccurate accusations, 'why are you touching me like that?'

'To gauge your reaction,' he told her. 'I need to see if you really are with me - to see if you mean what you say. I don't want to find I'm wasting more of my time.'

'You're not, Arthur,' she insisted meekly, 'but I'm not sure you should be touching me like that.'

'Then how would you like me to touch you?'

'No, no that's not what I meant.'

'I've known you for years, Emily, haven't I?'

'Yes...' Emily began to feel ashamed for questioning him.

'So you know you can trust me, don't you?'

'Yes... yes I suppose so.' Emily didn't move as Arthur eased his fingers a little deeper between her thighs and stroked the swell of her panties a little more deliberately. 'Arthur, I'm confused,' she confessed as he ran his free hand up her arm to her shoulder, then her cheeks flushed and she gasped sweetly as a fingertip managed to prise just between her sex lips.

'I know you are,' he breathed huskily, his hand starting to move rhythmically between the tightness of her closed thighs. 'That's why I'm doing this for you.'

'What do you mean?' she whispered. 'I... I don't want you to...'

'It's all right, Emily,' he encouraged, and his hand moved slowly down and pressed flat to the upper slope of one warm breast. 'Just trust me.'

Emily's thoughts were spinning, compounded by a nagging feeling that Arthur had touched her intimately before, after she'd drunk that wine. 'But...'

'Don't you trust me?' he pressed. 'After all these years we've been friends, don't you trust me?'

'Yes, yes I do,' she insisted desperately, not wanting to hurt the man's feelings. 'I suppose I'm still embarrassed though.'

'That's one of the things we're overcoming here,' he told her. 'Let's work together on this, Emily. Okay?'

Emily didn't know what to do or say for the best. 'Well, I... I suppose it's all right,' she said quietly.

He smiled and nodded. 'Good girl.'

Closing her eyes and relaxing her tensed thighs just a fraction as she felt his fingers moving more freely against her hidden sex lips, her face flushing, her breasts rising as she breathed deeply, she did her best not to protest. It was humiliating to be touched so blatantly, sitting in her underwear in her neighbour's kitchen, but she trusted Arthur. As he said, they'd known each other for years. If she couldn't relax with him, then she'd never feel relaxed with anyone. Finally letting herself go and trying to clear her mind, she had to admit that the feel of a man's fingers stroking her sex and a hand cupping and caressing her breast was very nice.

A battle began to rage in her tormented mind, and she felt as though she was drowning in confusion. She began to tremble, her secret excitement mounting, finding it difficult to believe she was allowing her next-door neighbour to stroke her sex through her panties and touch her breast through her bra. But, she consoled herself, this was part of her learning curve. As Arthur assured her, this wasn't sexual.

With the man's fingertips moving up and down against her sex, the movement causing his hand to stroke the sensitive flesh of her inner thighs, adding to her excitement, she knew her clitoris was stirring. How far would Arthur go? Was this stage of her education nearing completion? She could feel her love juices seeping into the crotch of her panties as he continued to probe with his fingertips against the dampening white cotton. And then she gasped, her moist lips parting slightly, as his hand crept from one breast to the other, and then moved so he could pinch her stiffening nipple through her bra.

'Is that nice?' Arthur asked, rolling the nipple between finger and thumb and squeezing the gentle swell of her vaginal lips.

Emily nodded.

'Good, you're doing very well,' he encouraged. 'And as you're being so good I have a present for you.'

'You have?' Emily murmured. 'What is it?'

'I'm not going to spoil the surprise,' he teased, and suddenly his hands withdrew and he stood up, adding to Emily's bewilderment. She opened her eyes and noticed the slightly distorted front of his trousers, only a foot or two from her flushed face. 'That's enough for now,' he said, and Emily realised she actually felt disappointed that his attentions were over. 'You go home and put on some dry clothes. Then come back here and we'll see what I've got for you. Okay?'

Emily nodded, then stood on rather shaky legs so he could slip his raincoat around her shoulders.

Chapter 12

Emily was aware of feeling excitement as she dried her hair after taking a warming shower. Then she put on some fresh white panties, her white bra and a light blouse and skirt.

She looked pretty, she reflected happily, gazing into her dressing table mirror, then standing and smoothing her skirt against her hips and thighs with her palms. Turning this way and that, she knew she looked good. She also felt good. Arthur's recent attentions seemed to liberate her feelings.

Wondering what the present was as she trotted down the stairs, she realised she'd lost all feelings of anxiety. He was harmless, she thought, leaving the house by the backdoor. Besides, deep down she'd rather enjoyed his intimate touches. Not that she'd admit it to him, she vowed as she walked up his garden path. The feel of his fingers against her sex and his hand on her breasts had been rather nice. But was it right? Deciding to relax and stop dwelling on things, to try and get the best from Arthur's help, she walked into his kitchen and called out.

'In here,' Arthur called back, and she found him in his lounge.

'You look lovely, Emily,' he said admiringly, looking her up and down. 'You're a lovely girl indeed.'

'Thank you,' she said coyly, blushing yet again. 'So, what's this present you've got for me?'

Arthur chuckled. 'Now, now, all in good time,' he chided good-humouredly. 'Would you like a glass of wine first?'

'In the middle of the day?' she giggled. 'Um, I don't think so, no.'

'Of course you would,' he goaded, moving to the sideboard and pouring her a glass. 'I chilled it earlier in readiness for our celebration.'

'Celebration?' she echoed, cocking her head to one side. 'What celebration?'

'All in good time, young lady, all in good time,' he teased again. 'I'm afraid I have a little bad news for you first. Your father rang.'

'Oh?' she said, her stomach sinking. 'What's wrong? Are they all right?'

'Yes, yes they're fine,' he said hastily.

'What's the bad news then?' she asked, accepting the glass of wine.

'He asked me whether you'd been out late at night.'

'And what did you tell him?' she asked anxiously.

'I said no, not at all, that I'd been mistaken when I thought you'd come home at two in the morning. I told him you're being very well behaved and have not been out, that you're spending most of your time studying.'

'Well someone must have said something to him,' she said warily. 'He wouldn't have asked unless someone had said something.'

'At a guess, I'd say he might have spoken to Christine,' he suggested. 'Perhaps she inadvertently let it slip.'

'Christine? No, she wouldn't...' her words tailing off, Emily frowned. 'Why would she do that? How *could* she do that? She doesn't know the name or number of their hotel.'

'Don't worry, I covered for you, just like I said I would,' he assured her. 'Your father's quite happy now he's talked to me about it. I will say this, though; I wouldn't tell Christine anything, if you know what I mean...' He looked at her meaningfully. 'She might let something else slip, something we definitely wouldn't want your parents knowing about.' He tapped the side of his nose conspiratorially.

'No, we wouldn't,' Emily agreed, thinking she knew what he was alluding to. 'I do wish my phone was working. Have they told you when it'll be fixed?'

'I've been onto the phone company and they're looking into it,' he told her. 'Perhaps, as your phone wasn't working, your father rang Christine. He might have called here when we were out and decided to ring her place to see whether you were there.'

'Yes, yes he must have done,' she agreed, nodding contemplatively. 'I thought Christine had been keeping a bit quiet. She's not been in touch for a while.'

'Now you know why. As I said, it would be best not to say anything to her about anything. We don't want anyone to know I'm helping you, now do we?'

'You've got me worried now,' Emily sighed, finishing her wine.

'I wasn't going to mention this,' he said, lowering his voice a little, 'but if I tell you something will you promise not to say anything to her?'

'What is it?' Emily asked, getting worried again.

'You must promise me.'

'Yes, yes I promise,' she said hurriedly, desperate for him to divulge whatever it was he had to say.

'She's not a good friend,' he stated flatly. 'She phoned me the other day.'

'Why?' the worried girl asked. 'What did she say?'

'She suggested that I make you stay in during the evenings,' he disclosed.

'She did *what?*' Emily squealed, aghast.

'Can't you guess why?'

'No, I can't.'

'Think about it, Emily. Why would Christine want you out of the way? You dwell on that while I refill your glass.'

Frowning, Emily couldn't think why Christine would do such a thing. But she was now sure the girl had spoken to her father. What was she trying to do? Why try to get her into trouble? Watching Arthur pouring the wine, she couldn't think of one reason why her best friend would want her out of the way. Unless... a terrible thought struck her.

'I take it you've worked it out,' he said, handing her back the refreshed glass.

'Because she's after Jack,' Emily said angrily. 'She wants me out of the way so she can have a free go at chatting up Jack.'

'As I said,' Arthur inveigled, sowing the necessary seeds, 'she's not a good friend. She obviously spoke to your father, and she's trying to get you apart from your young man. But remember what I said: don't mention anything about this to her.'

'Don't mention it?' she gasped. 'I'll kill her!'

'No, no, no,' he urged, shaking his head. 'Look at it like this; why does she want you out of the way?'

'Because she's after Jack.'

'Yes, but don't you see what that means?'

'I'm not with you.'

'A week ago Christine would have had no need to get you out of the way,' he reasoned. 'She'd have simply taken him from you.'

'What difference has a week made?' she asked, baffled.

'The week has made no difference, Emily,' he said. '*You've* made the difference.'

She pouted sulkily. 'I don't understand.'

'A week ago you were no threat to her,' he explained, smiling a little patronisingly at her. 'Now, with my help, you do pose a serious threat to her.'

'I see,' Emily reflected, the alcohol already taking effect again as she sipped more of the wine.

'When your parents first went away you accused me of trying to get you into trouble, when all I was trying to do was keep you *out* of trouble. Christine is the one trying to get you into trouble.'

'Yes, yes I can see that,' she agreed 'Although I'm annoyed with her, I must say that I'm rather pleased with myself. I never thought she would look upon me as a threat where lads were concerned.'

'And you'll pose more than a threat once you've completed your education,' Arthur added.

'Yes, I will,' she said. 'And I have you to thank for that. You've done all this for me, and I can't thank you enough.'

'It's not thanks I want,' Arthur said, his hooded eyes targeting the swell of her breasts for a fleeting second.

'Oh?' Emily looked puzzled.

'I mean, you don't have to thank me,' he clarified.

Emily found it incredible to think that Christine thought of her as a threat, and she reflected that without Arthur she'd have got nowhere and would have known nothing of her so-called friend's duplicity.

'Now I know what she's up to I'll be able to fight back,' she mused determinedly.

'No,' Arthur advised, 'be cautious. Don't try to run before you can walk. We've a long way to go with your education before you even start thinking about taking on someone as wily as Christine. The reason I told you not to mention this to her is because you don't want to let on that you know her game.'

'Yes, I see,' Emily said eagerly.

'Try not to have any contact with her for a while longer,' he told her. 'Fortunately your phone's not working, which could be a blessing in disguise, I think.'

'Yes, perhaps it could be,' she pondered.

'Keep away from the girl, Emily.'

'I will,' she agreed. 'But for how long, do you think?'

'That depends on you.'

'You mean, the more I learn from you the sooner I'll be ready?'

He nodded perfunctorily. 'Exactly. Now I just have to go up to my office and make a phone call,' he went on. 'While I'm gone you can open your present. It's in that bag on the occasional table. They're something to wear, but I'll say no more than that. Try them on and you can show me when I come back down.'

As he left the room and climbed the stairs, Emily opened the bag inquisitively, rummaged inside and pulled out several pairs of beautiful, slinky, white silk panties. They were lovely, but a little shocking. Why had Arthur bought them for her? It wasn't the kind of thing a male neighbour bought for the younger girl next-door. They felt gorgeously soft and sexy, but she could never wear them. Surely he couldn't expect her to? She'd be only too pleased to if he hadn't bought them, but he had, and that changed everything.

'What do you think?' Arthur asked as he returned. 'Aren't you going to try them on?'

'Arthur, I can't wear these,' she gasped, holding a skimpy pair up and thinking how lovely they were. 'You shouldn't have bought them for me.'

'Christine would wear them,' he said, smiling at her.

'How do you know that?'

'I know, believe me.'

'You mean you've actually seen her?'

He nodded. 'At your house, yes. She was sitting on the sofa one afternoon when I popped round to see your father. I was in the armchair opposite her and I caught a glimpse up her skirt. I could see clearly, Emily. She wore a pair of silk panties similar to those. So if you want to compete with her...'

Emily picked up another pair and admired them too.

'You don't have a problem with the panties, do you?' he probed.

'A problem?' she said. 'No I don't, because I'm not going to wear them.'

'You're not? That's a shame, after I went out and bought them especially for you.'

Emily felt terrible; they were so attractive, and it was sweet of him to buy them for her.

'Go on,' he urged insistently, 'why don't you just try them on? At least see whether they fit nicely.'

'Well, I suppose it couldn't do any harm...' she faltered.

'It's all right, Emily, no one will disturb us,' he goaded. 'You're quite safe here with me. You slip them on and I'll get another bottle of wine from the fridge.'

As Arthur went into the kitchen Emily pondered his words. He seemed to think her embarrassment had gone completely. Surely he must realise she couldn't wear them because he'd bought them. It was improper. And she definitely did not want to wear them in front of him. Even if he couldn't see them, the idea of him knowing she was wearing such intimate underwear that he'd bought for her was not right. But he was trying to help her, she mused, and if she was going to get any benefit from his help she'd have to work with him instead of against him. So taking a deep breath she hastily slipped her cotton panties down and off and one of the new, silky pairs on, smoothing down her skirt again. They felt deliciously wicked against her intimate flesh, and made her tummy somersault excitedly.

'Well?' he said, placing another bottle of wine on the occasional table. 'How do they fit?'

'I - I don't know,' Emily replied, blushing, too embarrassed to admit to the man how the silky underwear made her feel. 'I mean, they do feel nice, I think.'

'And how do they look on you?' he asked, sitting in one of his armchairs.

'Quite nice, I suppose,' she said shyly.

'Well, come here and show me.' he told her.

'Arthur, I...'

'What's the matter?'

'I suppose I'm embarrassed,' she confessed, in turmoil because she also didn't want to appear ungrateful to him. 'Perhaps I'll be less embarrassed in a few days and I can show you then.'

'We haven't got a few days to waste, Emily,' he countered sternly. 'Time is of the essence. Now don't be so silly. I bought them to help you, so I at least deserve to see that I didn't waste my money and time.'

Emily pouted anxiously. 'Please try to understand that this isn't easy for me,' she whispered.

'Of course I understand that,' he said comfortingly.

'I feel you're rushing me a little.' she told him.

'You're being silly, young lady,' he gently admonished. 'You have nothing to worry about. As I said, there's no one to disturb us and you're perfectly safe here with me.'

Emily absorbed his words for a few seconds, and then taking a deep breath and closing her eyes, she lifted her skirt and allowed the man to gaze at her new silk panties, trying to calm her confused emotions. It took a few seconds, but it wasn't too bad, she realised. And no one else would ever know what she'd done in Arthur's lounge. It would be their secret.

'Stand with your feet just a little apart,' Arthur coaxed her gently. 'And lift your skirt a little higher. I want to make sure they fit snugly.'

'I think that's enough for now,' Emily murmured.

'We're almost done,' Arthur said reassuringly. 'Just turn around so I can see how they fit your bottom too.'

Obeying, Emily nervously nibbled her lower lip as Arthur leaned closer for a better view of her shapely buttocks filling the tight, shimmering fabric. Her stomach churning, her heart racing, she did her best to convince herself that this was the right thing to do, wondering what her next-door neighbour was thinking, managing to suppress an objection as he reached out and fleeting caressed one smooth, silk-encased buttock.

'They're perfect,' Arthur decided as Emily completed a full turn. 'Are they comfortable?'

'Yes, I think so,' she replied shakily. 'Arthur, I...'

'What is it?' he asked. 'You do like them, don't you? You look lovely in them.'

'Yes, yes,' she assured him, 'it's just that...'

'Come here and sit on my lap, Emily,' he beckoned, and she hesitated.

'All right,' she eventually said, lowering herself onto him.

'Okay, tell me what's on your mind,' he urged, placing his hand on her naked knee.

'Well, I'm not really sure,' she said, blushing furiously as she felt something solid pressing up against her bottom. 'I suppose it's thinking about Christine.'

'What about her?'

'She's not a virgin,' she disclosed.

'And you are,' he stated, gazing at the way her delicious breasts filled her blouse so beautifully, mere inches from his face. 'Is that what's bothering you?'

'Yes, it is,' she admitted, blushing and trying to ignore his blatant stare. 'I mean, I don't want to lose my virginity just because she has. But I suppose, what with the way she's let me down, I now realise just how gullible I am. And once she has Jack in her clutches that will be that.'

The man said nothing, letting her talk, his eyes still watching the movement of those firm breasts as she breathed.

'Look at me,' she sighed. 'I'm sitting here wearing silky underwear bought for me by an old friend of my parents. I don't know what's happened to me since they went on holiday. I can't help feeling this is wrong.'

'Go on,' he encouraged.

'Well, something inside is telling me this isn't right. I've got a nagging feeling I'm making a big mistake.'

'Keep talking, Emily,' he said firmly, looking serious. 'It'll do you good to get all this off your chest,' he added, and his eyes glanced at the extremely mouth-watering chest in question.

'When you first spanked me I couldn't believe it,' she confessed. 'But I realised you were only trying to keep me out of trouble. I must admit that I went a bit wild for the first few days. I suppose it was having a taste of freedom at last.'

'Relax, Emily,' he soothed, caressing her thigh. 'Close your eyes and relax.'

'No,' she gasped as his hand crept higher, slipped beneath her skirt, and again his fingers pressed against the front of her silk panties. 'Arthur, I...'

'Relax,' he said again, his voice hypnotic, his free arm around her waist, the hand surreptitiously pulling her skirt up around her hips, 'you're all wound up and tense.'

'This isn't right,' she objected as a finger delved into the moist groove between her sex lips. 'Arthur, please...'

'Of course it's right,' he coaxed. 'You need to relax, and I can help you.'

Her young body trembling as Arthur pressed deeper between her thighs, locating and massaging the sensitive nub of her swelling clitoris, Emily couldn't believe she'd trapped herself into this situation again. To allow him to touch her there was not right, despite what he said. She should never have agreed to wear the sexy panties, she reflected, closing her thighs and trapping his hand. She should never have sat on his lap. But she didn't want to upset him. Oh, how had she got herself into such a mess?

'You're not relaxing,' Arthur murmured, his finger encircling her yearning clitoris through the soft white silk.

'Arthur, I don't think you should—'

'Don't you like it?' he cut in. 'Doesn't it feel nice when I touch you like this?'

Emily gasped and her cheeks reddened. 'Yes, no... I mean... oh, I don't know.'

'All right,' he said, moving his hand back to her knee, 'if you don't want me to help relax you like that.'

'I do want to relax,' she complained. 'It's just, with you touching me I feel even more confused. Anyway, you said none of this was a sexual thing.'

'I don't think I like what you're suggesting, young lady,' he said sternly.

'I'm sorry,' she said hurriedly, 'but what you were doing to me was a sexual thing.'

'No, it wasn't,' he corrected her. 'Allow me to explain. You masturbate, don't you?'

Emily pouted shamefully. 'Well, yes, unfortunately you know I do.'

'You masturbate because your natural sexual urges build and you need to quell them. But when you masturbate it's not sex, as such. It's simply a matter of satisfying your urges. And that's all I was trying to do for you. It wasn't something sexual. Your thinking is all wrong, Emily.'

'How?' she asked.

'I was just trying to help you relax. It's not sex, it's me being aware of your inner turmoil and trying to help you, and what you're implying hurts me.'

Feeling more confused than ever Emily thought she understood what Arthur was getting at, but she found it difficult to look upon him touching her like he did as nothing to do with sex. Despite her shame and reservations she was secretly feeling really excited, and she desperately needed the release of an orgasm, but to allow Arthur to masturbate her didn't seem right at all. No one had ever touched her intimately before, she reflected, and she'd never, ever in a million years thought her next-door neighbour would be the first to do so. It was wrong, wasn't it? Just like wearing silk panties bought for her by her neighbour had to be wrong.

Arthur smoothed down her skirt again and ushered her to her feet. 'I think you'd better go now, Emily,' he said, suddenly cool towards her. 'You need to have a good long think about what you really want.'

'You know what I want,' she sighed with frustration. 'I just want to have more fun with my friends without my parents watching every move I make.'

'And to date Jack,' he observed candidly.

'Well,' she pouted, 'I do like him; you know that. Is that a crime?' she asked rhetorically. 'My parents would think it was.'

'They're only concerned for your well-being,' he said. 'You can't blame them for caring about you.'

'No, I can't, but—'

'Would you prefer it if they didn't care?'

'No... no of course I wouldn't, but that's not the—'

'And behaving as you have been with me, I'd forget any ideas of ever dating Jack if I were you.'

'What?' she gasped. 'Why do you say that?'

'Because Christine's winning hands down,' he stated. 'Carry on as you are doing and she'll win Jack and you'll miss out.'

'What do you mean?' she asked despondently. 'You said how well I was doing. You said I'm a serious threat to Christine.'

'Here's a little scenario for you,' he went on, ignoring her point. 'You're on a date with Jack. When you get a quiet moment together and start kissing and canoodling he slips his hand between your legs, his fingers touch you there,' he nodded towards her groin, 'but you go all coy and tell him to stop. Do you think he'll stick around when he knows he can get what he wants from Christine?'

'Well, I...' she was at a loss for what to say.

'That's what happened just now, Emily,' he pressed on cruelly. 'That's how you reacted and I was only trying to help you.' He shook his head dolefully. 'No, I think you'd better forget about Jack. Leave him to Christine. She knows what he wants. You're way out of your league.'

'But I thought the whole idea was that you'd help me,' she said.

'Ah, yes,' he sighed, 'but I've reconsidered. Now I think there's little point.'

'You seem so negative now,' she said miserably. 'You were all for it before.'

'Clearly I was wrong, Emily. Yes, I did think you were doing well, until I've noted your reactions whenever I touch you.'

'Arthur, you've had your hands between my legs, touching my sex,' she objected. 'And you've touched my breasts, too. That's a sexual thing, there's no denying it. How do you expect me to react?'

'Oh, you're just not willing to listen or learn, are you?' He rose and stood with his back to the unlit fireplace. 'I may have touched you like you said - although I would be *extremely* unhappy if you told anyone else about that,' he warned, 'but that is to help you. It is not a sexual thing, as I have told you enough times before.' The man tutted and shook his head. 'And now I think we'd better forget about me offering you help and advice. I'm not prepared to have you question my motives, young lady. I'm extremely disappointed that you could even think such a thing, let alone voice it.'

'So what do you want from me?' Emily asked, exasperated. 'Do you want me to take my panties off and allow you to masturbate me?'

Arthur watched her for a few seconds, his stare level and unblinking. 'Yes,' he said, 'if you still want me to help you, that's exactly what I want.'

'And do eighteen year old girls usually allow older men to do that to them?' she challenged.

'No, they usually allow youths to fumble and grope and make a complete mess of things,' he said scornfully. 'Look, I have a lot of work to do. I've already given up enough of my time for you but you don't seem to appreciate that fact, so I think we'll go back to the way things were.'

'The way things were?' Despite her confusion regarding Arthur's motives, Emily felt crestfallen that he was giving up on her.

'Yes, we'll do it your parents' way,' he told her. 'They don't want you going out in the evenings, so we'll abide by their wishes and you'll have to stay in at night and study instead.'

Emily didn't know what to say. Why was Arthur doing this? He wanted to masturbate her, she mused. That's what this was all about, and because she wouldn't allow him to touch her in that way she was to stay in and rot while her friends were out enjoying themselves. It was blackmail, wasn't it? Was it right to allow a man of his age to touch her? Her next-door neighbour, a good family friend; he'd be demanding sex with her next...

'I'm going home,' she said dejectedly, moving to the lounge door. 'I think I'll get down to some studying right now.'

'Good idea,' Arthur agreed. 'And remember that you're not to go out later.'

'So I'm grounded,' she concluded. 'Is that what you're saying?'

Arthur nodded. 'Emily, it's not me, not my doing.

'We're back to the report book then?'

'We are, yes,' he confirmed. 'We're back to square one. You can't have it both ways.'

'The report book - you'll have to change it again,' she pointed out.

'It's as it was, Emily,' he admitted. 'I hadn't got round to changing it so it will stay as it was.'

'But...' She faltered, unsure whether to voice any more thoughts.

'But what?' he encouraged.

'This is blackmail,' she accused.

'Oh dear, we really are back to square one, aren't we?'

'What you're saying is that I'll be allowed out if I let you touch me,' she said frankly. 'In my book that's blackmail.'

Arthur watched her closely and then came to a decision. 'Come with me, there's something I want to show you.'

Following him upstairs, Emily wondered what he was up to now, and gasped as he opened the door to his spare bedroom and she saw the wooden chair positioned in the centre of the floor. It was completely devoid of any other furniture.

'What's that for?' she asked, fearing she knew the answer all too well as he placed a hand on her shoulder, ushered her inside and closed and locked the door behind them, as though cutting her off from the outside world completely.

'I told you I was preparing a little surprise for you, now bend over the back of the chair,' he instructed forthrightly, straight to the point.

'No,' she objected, shaking her head in trepidation, 'this isn't right—'

'You'll only make it worse for yourself if you argue,' he snapped, his mood alarming her. 'Surely you've learned that much by now.'

'Why are you going to punish me?' she asked.

'Because we're starting again, from square one,' he told her uncompromisingly.

'But I haven't done anything wrong,' she demurred. 'I've already said that I'll be staying in and studying. Besides, you don't have your silly evidence against me now. The photographs are—'

'In a safe place,' he cut in, his lips curling into a sly smile. 'Bend over the chair, Emily.'

'You lied to me,' she gasped. 'You said you'd destroyed them.'

'Yes, I lied to you,' he confirmed.

'I thought we were getting on so well,' she complained desperately. 'I thought you were my friend, that you were going to help me.'

'Bend over the back of the chair, young lady,' he ordered determinedly. 'You don't want me to ring your father, do you? Please, let's not go through all that again.'

Eyeing the locked door and reluctantly accepting her fate, knowing it was useless to rebel, she leant forward over the piece of furniture forlornly, closed her eyes and grimaced as he folded her skirt up over her back and pulled her new panties down to her knees. She thought she'd known confusion before, but nothing compared to this. With a myriad thoughts battering her tormented mind as her neighbour ran his fingertips over the naked flesh of her rounded buttocks, she didn't know what to do for the best any more.

'Number one,' Arthur growled, the palm of his hand meeting the taut flesh of Emily's naked bottom with a resounding slap. Her young body jerking with each gruelling strike, the chair creaking as it rocked beneath her, she bravely uttered not a sound as tears welled in her eyes. She couldn't win, she knew, her glowing buttocks stinging as Arthur continued the merciless spanking.

Pinning her down as she tried to stand upright after the sixth, he spanked her even harder for her futile show of rebellion. With the pain becoming intense as the brute continued to pound the naked globes of her stinging bottom, the bending girl could suppress a pitiful sob no longer. Her tensed body trembling uncontrollably, she prayed for him to halt the gruelling punishment. She couldn't endure much more, she knew, as tears blurred her eyes and dripped onto the seat of the chair beneath her red face.

'No more,' she sobbed, her lovely new panties now stretched around her ankles. 'I can't take any more.' And to her surprise he actually did desist and let her stand so she could rub her scorched rear.

'All right,' he relented, breathing a little heavily from the exertion, 'that's enough for now. But you'll behave yourself properly in my house, have you got that?'

'I have behaved myself,' she sulked. 'Just because I wouldn't allow you to touch me like you want to.'

'You still don't understand, do you?' he snapped. 'This has nothing to do with me. But I can't waste any more time trying to explain that to you. I'm going to get on with some work now. Call me if you need anything.'

'You can't leave me shut in here,' Emily protested, pulling her panties back up, wincing as they touched her scalded bottom.

'I have no choice,' Arthur said dismissively. 'Now we're back to doing things your father's way I'm going to have to keep my eye on you.'

'This is ridiculous,' she complained. 'Whatever I do I can't win.'

'This isn't a game, Emily,' he stated grimly. 'As I once said, there are no winners. You're going to have to decide once and for all what it is you want. I'll leave you to contemplate that. Think hard, young lady. Think hard.'

Listening to the door being locked from the outside, Emily gazed out of the window at the garden, and with her buttocks throbbing she wondered whether she should yield to the man. It might well make her life a whole lot less complicated if she did.

'Arthur,' she called, banging on the locked door as she quickly came to a decision. 'Arthur, I need to talk to you.'

'What is it?' he asked impatiently, unlocking and opening the door. 'What is it? I'm trying to get on with some work.'

'Arthur...' Emily took a deep breath and summoned every ounce of courage she had. 'I... I agree,' she said tentatively

'You agree to what?' he pressed, apparently with little interest.

'I agree to allow you to do whatever you deem necessary to help educate me,' she conceded. 'If you still want to help me, that is.'

Arthur studied her for long, tense moments. 'You'd better come downstairs,' he said sternly, clearly still disillusioned with her. 'I think we need to have a serious talk about this.'

'There's nothing to talk about,' she said, following him back down the stairs to the lounge. 'I've come to a decision, and that's that.'

'Sit down, Emily,' he ordered. 'Now, firstly,' he started once she was sitting on his sofa, her face grimacing against the sore contact. 'You must understand once and for all that I wasn't doing what I was doing - touching you like I did - for my own benefit or gratification. You have to get that silly notion out of your head, otherwise far from me being able to help you, to become your ally, we'll both end up in trouble. Loose talk would be extremely dangerous. Do you understand me?'

'I'm sorry,' she meekly apologised, feeling guilty for the things she'd accused him of. 'I didn't mean any offence, and I don't want to get you in any trouble.'

'It's not what *I* want, Emily,' he insisted. 'I was doing what I did for you, to help you. Not for me.'

'Give me all the photographs and clean the others off your computer, and we'll be friends again,' she said.

'Ah, so that's what this is all about,' he mused.

'I don't want any trouble when my parents get home,' she said, 'so you win.'

'I can't give you the photographs,' he announced.

'Why not? I'm agreeing to...'

'Because I've already destroyed them,' he told her. 'I only told you I still had them to concentrate your mind.'

'Concentrate my mind?'

'Because I've been getting nowhere with you, Emily. Whatever I've tried to do you've battled against me.'

'Well I'm not battling now.'

'So what is it you want?'

Emily thought for a while, then admitted, 'I don't know what I want. I'm mixed up. I'm confused about Christine, I'm confused about Jack, I'm confused about you, I'm confused about everything. I don't know what I want, or what to do for the best.'

'Discipline, Emily,' he stated. 'You need discipline.'

'No, not another spanking,' she pleaded. 'I couldn't take any more.'

'I know it's not easy for you to agree to discipline after years without it.'

'Without it?' she protested.

'You might have a strict father,' he conceded, 'but you've certainly not been properly disciplined. Discipline isn't just a matter of doing what you're told, you know. There's far more to it than that.'

'All right, I'll do it,' she agreed.

'Do what?'

'Allow you to discipline me.'

Arthur shook his head. 'It's not simply a case of that.'

'Arthur, I've come to a decision,' she repeated. 'Please don't make this more difficult for me than it already is. I'm in your hands again now. I'm putting myself completely in your hands.'

'Why, Emily?' he enquired, eyeing her closely. 'Why have you suddenly decided this?'

'Because I'm fed up and I want to change things,' she explained. 'Just tell me what it is you want me to do; what it is you want from me.'

Arthur rubbed his chin pensively. 'Before we go any further,' he said, 'I must be sure you mean what you say, that you're not going to waste even more of my time.'

'I won't waste your time, I promise,' she said. 'Just tell me what you want me to do.' Emily knew she really had given in, had put herself in the hands of her next-door neighbour. Was she doing the right thing? He'd manipulated her, she reflected. He'd manipulated her and the situation, using his convoluted psychology to ensnare her. She sensed that, but still she went with it.

'This is your last chance, Emily,' he warned her. 'You do understand that, don't you?'

'Yes, I understand,' she replied.

'Whatever happens from hereon in, it's your decision, yes?'

'Yes,' she whispered breathlessly. 'Just tell me what to do.'

The man ruminated for a while longer. 'Very well, young lady,' he eventually said. 'But as we've wasted a number of days I'm going to throw you in at the deep end. Take your skirt and blouse off.'

'Do I have to?' she asked, immediately realising she was in danger of falling at the first hurdle.

'I told you to remove your blouse and skirt,' he snapped. 'Do it, or have I just spent the last ten minutes listening to insincere, time-wasting platitudes?'

Unbuttoning her blouse, Emily felt her face blushing as she dropped it onto the sofa. With her nipples stirring shamefully she sat coyly before her neighbour in her skirt and bra. It was embarrassing in the extreme, but now she was committed to doing exactly as Arthur said.

'You do agree to this?' he asked her again, his eyes moving from her face to her breasts, and then back up again.

'Yes,' she answered softly.

'You agree to put yourself in my hands utterly?'

She nodded.

'Good,' he smiled, 'then I think we're getting somewhere at last.'

Emily nodded, despite being less confident than him about that.

'Are you aroused, my dear?' he suddenly asked, catching the girl completely by surprise.

'No,' she gasped. 'I... no.'

'Are you sure about that?' he pressed. 'I want an honest answer; are you aroused?'

'Yes,' she said, responding to his first question and instantly realising that sounded wrong. 'I mean, no.'

'You want me to lie to your parents, don't you?'

'Lie?'

'That's what it amounts to, if I cover for you,' he said. 'You know how much I hate lying, yet you want me to hide your clothes here so you can sneak round and get changed before going out without their knowledge.'

Emily felt ashamed having it spelled out to her so frankly. 'Yes, I suppose I do.' How far, she wondered, was this going to go? If she allowed Arthur to touch her, if it was all a part of her 'education', would he expect her to touch him in return? No, surely not. That was unthinkable, ridiculous, and she banished the thought from her head. She had to keep Arthur on her side, and that meant dismissing ideas that would anger him if he knew she was having them. Whatever happened she had to keep Arthur on her side, she repeated the mantra over and over in her head.

'Take off your skirt,' he ordered her, and without question, knowing it had to be done, she stood, slipped out of the light garment, and again sat meekly on the front edge of the sofa, her stomach churning nervously as he joined her there. 'Now, are you ready?' he asked.

Emily took a deep breath, her breasts filling her bra deliciously, squeezing her cleavage tight. 'Yes, I think so,' she whispered.

As Arthur's hand lifted from his thigh and cupped the smooth firmness of her left breast Emily stiffened, closely watching his expression. He squeezed several times, and then his fingers moved, fastening to her nipple through the lacy white cup, pinching, pulling and rolling, and she tried to convince herself that he was doing this to help her and that she was enjoying it. This was all part of the discipline, she told herself, to check her responses, to confirm her acceptance of his methods. This was all for her own good. It had nothing to do with sex, or with Arthur's own gratification. It was to help her, nothing more.

'You're doing very well,' Arthur drawled, his fingertips encircling the protruding outline of her erect nipple. 'Are you enjoying it?'

'I... yes,' she confessed in hushed, uncertain tones, not wanting to displease the man.

'Good girl,' he cajoled, and as he moved to her right breast Emily felt her stomach somersault again. The feel of him touching her wasn't at all unpleasant, she secretly admitted. The concept of her older neighbour touching her was still alien, but the physical reality was rather exciting - though she was ashamed to admit it to herself, let alone to him. The nagging doubt that this was wrong still tugged at her conscience. Arthur was old enough to be her... he was a similar age to her father. But he was experienced and he was sharing that experience to teach her - to help her. It would be obtuse and ungrateful of her not to match his efforts.

As Arthur stroked her nipples and massaged her firm, youthful breasts, Emily felt her clitoris stirring between her wet sex lips, her juices of arousal seeping between the engorged petals into her new silk panties. Knowing an orgasm would result if Arthur carried on touching her, she began to secretly hope he would, even though she was still torn between what was right and what was wrong.

'Now,' he said, his voice quiet, a little husky, 'I'm going to take your bra off,' he told her, and her breath catching in her throat, she was unable to voice any response.

He watched her closely for any signs of another rebellion, and seeing none he embraced her and fiddled with the fastening behind her back. It took him a few attempts, but eventually the bra straps slackened as the catch came free, and he leaned back to watch the flimsy lace fall away and admired the way her naked breasts sprang free, not even the slightest hint of any sag, the cleavage still deep and inviting even without the constrictions of the bra.

'Beautiful,' he murmured, the compliment making her blush just as much as the blatant admiration of her naked breasts did. 'You are truly beautiful, Emily.' With his eyes fixed to her delicious fruits, he untangled the bra from her wrist and left it discarded between them.

'Now, don't move,' he ordered, and she watched, mesmerised, as he slowly leaned forward and kissed one of her nipples. She gasped and almost moved back away from him, but remained steadfast, her back straight and her shoulders held proudly as his mouth opened and he sucked the nipple into his mouth. He was watching her, looking up into her face to catch any warning signs of a mutiny. Even at this stage he was taking nothing for granted.

'Arthur,' she whispered, her thoughts in turmoil, 'are you sure about this?'

'You're in my hands,' he said, releasing her erect, glistening nipple from his mouth, 'and it's too late now for any doubts. There's no going back now, Emily. You know that as much as I do.'

'Perhaps, but—'

'There's no perhaps about it,' he stopped her, placing a fingertip to her lips silencing her with his stare. 'That's better,' he went on. 'Now, no more silliness please, young lady. You've put yourself in my hands, and there's no going back.'

He waited a few more seconds, and then sucked her other nipple between his lips. He nipped with his teeth causing Emily to inhale sharply, arching her back, inadvertently feeding more of her succulent breast into his grateful mouth. He sucked and licked and gnawed, the bud growing under the avaricious attention.

'Arthur, you shouldn't be doing this,' she sighed ineffectually, and he possessively mauled her other breast and slipped an arm around her waist to pull her even closer to him. Her head lolled back, her breast becoming wetter with his saliva as he devoured more of the smooth flesh, trying to get as much of it into his mouth as he could.

Then he pulled away and stared at her again. 'You're not going to change your mind again, are you?' he challenged.

'N-no,' Emily sighed.

'Good girl.' He slipped one hand back beneath a cushion and produced the short length of white rope. 'But let's just help you keep to that conviction, shall we?

Emily eyed the rope warily. 'Really, there's no need to do that.'

'Maybe,' he mused, 'maybe not. But I always think a little insurance never goes amiss.'

Emily said no more, and obeyed resignedly as he told her to cross her wrists and twist her torso a little so he could wrap the rope around them a few times and bind them securely together.

'You're doing very well, my dear,' he repeated, putting his hands on her shoulders and turning her back to face him, admiring her naked, vulnerable breasts. 'I'm pleased with your progress.'

'You're not going to spank me again, are you?' she asked timidly, knowing by now that the rope usually signified just that. 'My bottom's still sore from the last time.'

'No, Emily,' he smiled, 'I'm not going to spank you again. For the moment, at least,' he added.

'You're a virgin, Emily,' he went on, his hands stroking her shoulders, then down to her upper arms.

'Yes,' she confirmed, uneasily aware that her breasts were completely at the mercy of his whims, 'I've already told you that.'

'I know you have, but I just want to be sure.' He stood up in front of her. 'Christine has so many advantages over you,' he stated, 'so it's time we levelled the playing field somewhat.'

'Arthur, what do you mean?' she asked anxiously, uncomfortably aware of his groin hovering level with her face. 'I don't think that I...'

'You've never seen a penis before, have you?' he asked.

'No!' she gasped indignantly. 'No I haven't.'

'Are you sure, Emily?'

'Yes, of course I'm sure,' she insisted.

'Then I think a lesson in male anatomy is required.'

'Arthur...'

'Just answer yes or no from now on, Emily.'

As he moved closer, the obviously distended crotch of his trousers now mere inches from her horrified face, Emily felt her stomach churn. Was his penis erect? Judging by the way his trousers were obscenely distorted he definitely was. Did he intend to masturbate in front of her? Surely not.

'Tell me your thoughts,' Arthur coaxed, his hands hovering dangerously close to the fastenings of his trousers.

'I... I don't know what they are,' she replied shakily but truthfully.

'You do want to go ahead with your tuition, don't you?'

'No, I...' she faltered confusedly. 'There's no need for this.'

'No need?' he echoed. 'Let me be the judge of that, young lady. You've placed yourself in my hands, you trust me to do what's right for you, so how can you say there's no need for this?'

'Arthur, you're the same age as my father,' she pointed out desperately.

'What has my age got to do with anything?' he asked.

'I don't know, but...'

'That's the point, Emily,' he said, 'you don't know. You don't know anything. You're eighteen years old and you're still a virgin. You see how you're reacting? What will Jack think if you hesitate and shy away from him like this? Given the chance Christine won't, be sure about that. If you don't grow up she'll steal him away from you as easily as that,' and he clicked his fingers to emphasise his point. 'You have no choice but to trust me and press on, Emily.'

'But Arthur, I'm—'

'Don't you trust me?'

'It's not that,' she said. 'It's just that I...'

As he slid his zip down and a hand delved inside his trousers, Emily couldn't drag her wide eyes away from it. Despite her horror she watched spellbound, and then her heart leapt into her throat and she instinctively licked her lips as the man pulled his erect penis out into the open. Warily eyeing the purple glans pulsing only inches from her burning face, she gasped as he rummaged inside his clothing again and then dragged his balls out too. This couldn't be right, she thought, as he lewdly stroked a fist up and down the length of his cock a few times. He was supposed to be keeping an eye on her; to show her his penis like this was the last thing she'd ever expected.

'It's not so bad, is it?' he said. 'It's not frightening, is it?'

'Um, no, I don't suppose so,' she breathed softly.

'Your first ever look at a penis,' he stated, 'but there has to be a first time for everything. So what do you think?'

'I don't know,' she whispered, unable to take her eyes off the semi-erect column of veined flesh bobbing out from his open trousers.

'Take a good look at it,' he encouraged. 'Take your time and examine it properly.'

Gazing at his purple crown, Emily realised he wouldn't have tied her hands behind her back if he was going to make her masturbate him, which was a relief. But even so, she couldn't believe her next-door neighbour was standing before her exposing himself like this. What else did he intend?

'I can't do it,' she sighed, lowering her head.

'You can't do what?' he asked her. 'I've not asked you to do anything.'

'I can't do any of this,' she whispered. 'I'm sorry, but I can't do any of it.'

'You disappoint me, young lady,' he said brusquely, tutting and shaking his head as he prised his penis back into his trousers and hauled his zip up. 'I'm doing this for you, for your benefit.'

'I know, and I'm grateful for that,' she said. 'But it's all too much too soon.'

'We don't have a great deal of time, that's why I'm pushing you,' he reminded her. 'For goodness sake, girl, whatever is the matter with you? One minute you beg for my help, and then you go all silly on me again. It really is too much. You're messing me around and I don't like it.'

'I'm sorry, but it's all too much,' she sobbed, hanging her head in shame.

'You asked me not to beat you again,' he said ominously, 'but then you behave like this and leave me with little other choice.

'What?' she shrieked. 'No, you can't, please.'

'Come on,' he said, ignoring her pleas as he grabbed her by the elbow and hauled her unceremoniously to her feet, her breasts quivering as he pushed her forward out of the lounge and up the stairs. 'Get up there. We're going to sort this out once and for all.'

On the landing, both of them panting from the exertion of him bundling her up the stairs, Arthur threw open the door of the spare bedroom.

Chapter 13

'Bend over the chair again,' he growled, pushing her in, roughly pulling her skirt up as she obediently leant over, and tugging her panties down to her knees. 'I was trying to help you, but yet again you throw it back in my face.'

'I didn't mean too,' she protested, finding it a strain to maintain her position with her hands still bound behind her back, the top of the chair digging uncomfortably into her lower tummy. 'It was just that—'

'I'm going to thrash some respect and good manners into you, young lady,' he threatened. 'I've just about had enough of your petulant, ungrateful behaviour.'

'Arthur, please...' she beseeched the man.

'At least that's a good start,' he said, removing his leather belt from the loops of his trousers. 'It's about time you showed some contrition. And now you'll really plead with me.'

The belt swept down through the air and Emily shrieked as it struck the tensed flesh of her naked bottom with a sickening crack. There was a brief pause while he raised his arm again, and then the leather bit into the stinging globes a second time, wrapping round to cause havoc in her flank too, the strap following the curvature of her quivering body. Emily again cried out, but her plaintive cries only fuelled Arthur's anger and he whipped her again with a vengeance. Her body jerking with every gruelling lash, she knew he wasn't going to show any leniency this time. She'd gone too far. She'd misled him yet again.

Incensed, he repeatedly brought the leather belt down across the glowing orbs of her naked bottom. With the leather biting into the backs of her shapely thighs too, she knew he'd be able to see the lips of her pussy peeping between them. Was his penis still erect? Did he want to have sex with her? With the leather belt snapping through the air, repeatedly flailing her poor defenceless bottom, she again begged him to stop.

Eventually feeling his fingertips running over her fiery buttocks as he lowered the belt to his side, she prayed the thrashing was over. He'd administered a dozen or so lashes, she pondered as tears filled her eyes. Was he finished with her? She wasn't sure as he stroked the crimsoned flesh of her ravaged bottom. He was teasing her, taunting her. Lifting her skirt higher, he ran his fingertips over the blotchy welts he'd created on her otherwise unblemished flesh, and around the small tattoo adorning her beaten buttock.

Squeezing her eyes shut as his fingers delved into the valley of her bottom, she dare not utter one word of protest. He had already shown her his bamboo cane and she didn't want to provoke him into using that on her too. To rile him further now would be asking for real trouble. As his fingertips actually teased the sensitive little star of her anus she let out a rush of breath, wondering what he was doing. How far would he go? Why was he touching her there? His fingertip pressed and she held her breath, utterly bemused by the action. Would he move his finger down to the moist entrance of her vagina? If he did try to penetrate her, dare she attempt to stop him?

The fingers withdrew and the leather belt again cut through the air and lashed her tensed buttocks with a horrendous crack. Emily screamed piteously. Arthur wasn't going to relent, she knew, as the belt repeatedly flailed her glowing flesh. With crack after crack resounding around the room Emily tried to stand up to halt the onslaught, but Arthur pinned her down with his free hand. She pictured her red-raw flesh as the belt whipped her again and again. She'd not be able to sit down for days, the pain permeating her young bottom.

'Please,' she cried, the glowing orbs of her bottom tensing uncontrollably.

'That'll be enough for the time being,' Arthur finally relented, allowing her to wearily lift her trembling form upright. 'But you'll have another taste of the belt before you leave this house, believe me.'

'Please, no,' she whimpered. 'I can't take any more.'

'Whether you can take it or not, you're going to get it. When are you going to learn, Emily? How many times do I have to tell you to behave yourself properly?'

'I'm sorry,' she sobbed. 'Really, I'm sorry.'

'So you'll show me due respect and do things my way?' he demanded.

'I... I suppose so,' she conceded, gingerly comforting her smarting buttocks.

'You suppose so?' he echoed. 'Not good enough, Emily. Will you or won't you?'

'Yes,' she said, pouting as her hot bottom throbbed, warily eyeing the leather belt swinging menacingly from his hand, its threatening presence making her forget her naked breasts, 'I will do things your way, if I must.'

'If think you can change your mind again...' Arthur warned, wagging a finger at her.

'No, I won't,' she promised. 'I'll do exactly as you say. I promise.'

'No more rebelling?' he said. 'No more questioning my methods and motives?'

'No, none of that,' she promised meekly.

'All right, but be warned that I will not tolerate any more bad behaviour whatsoever. I will not tolerate it, do you hear me?'

'Yes, I hear you,' she confirmed.

'Good,' he said, satisfied. 'Then kneel on the floor.'

'Kneel?'

'Yes, kneel before me.'

Wondering what he had in mind for her now, Emily obeyed and looked up at the looming man as he stared down at her. What was he thinking? What was he planning to do? She felt humbled as he stroked her tearstained cheek with his free hand, the belt dangling ominously close by.

'Do you pledge to accept the help I offer you without question?' he asked her, 'and to show me the respect I deserve?'

'Yes, I do,' she said, wondering what this was all about.

'Do you promise to obey without further argument or protest?'

'I...' she wavered, then took a deep breath to calm her anxieties, 'yes, I do.'

'Stand up, Emily,' he instructed, and when she did, a little awkwardly with her wrists still bound together behind her back, she held her breath and watched his free hand as it slowly lifted and cupped her breast, his thumb rolling across her erect nipple, causing her to gasp and her stomach to lurch pleasantly. Wondering deep down whether succumbing to her next-door neighbour in this way was the right thing to do, she remained obediently quiet and motionless as he moved his

109

hand to squeeze and knead her other breast as well.

'I'm going to untie your wrists now,' he told her, 'and then you will pull up your panties but remove your skirt and come downstairs.' He turned Emily around and she felt his fingers loosening the knot binding her arms together. When they were free she rubbed her wrists to bring relief to them and turned to watch him leave the room. 'Downstairs, quickly,' he said over his shoulder.

Emily looked down at her skirt and hesitated. What, she wondered, was he planning to do now? Did he want to seduce her? Was that what he'd wanted all along? No, surely not: this was Arthur, long-term friend of the family. Resignedly she bent to pull up her panties, gasping a little as even the delicate silk irritated her scorched buttocks, then unfastened the skirt at her waist, allowed it to whisper down her legs, and elegantly stepped out of the crumpled garment.

Then muttering words of courage to herself, she left the bedroom and hesitantly made her way down the stairs to the lounge.

'Good girl,' Arthur praised her as she stood in the doorway, looking absolutely beautiful and humble in just her white panties, the smooth silk swelling slightly over her sex mound tight between her thighs, her hands uselessly at her sides. 'Come and stand in front of me,' he beckoned as he sat in his armchair. 'That's better,' he smiled up at her when she had positioned herself just in front of his knees, 'now I can see you properly.

'So, Emily,' he proceeded, 'are you feeling comfortable enough, standing before me with just your panties on?'

'Well, I suppose so, I think,' she said quietly. 'Although to be honest I still feel embarrassed.'

'You will for a while, that's only natural,' he conceded. 'But this is all towards teaching you vital discipline, my girl. Doing as I say when I say is helping you learn obedience. One who is humble is also obedient. And in return, before your parents get back from their holiday you may bring all your new clothes round here. I have a spare wardrobe you can use.'

'Thank you,' Emily said.

'If ever you want to go out with your friends you can change here and I'll drop you off in town, and then I'll pick you up when you're ready to come home.'

Pondering the plan, Emily believed it would work. She'd go to Arthur's house dressed in her jeans, and then change into her party clothes. He'd drop her off at the wine bar, bring her home later, and her parents would be none the wiser. And her holiday in Tenerife would even be salvaged; not that she wanted to go on holiday with traitorous Christine any more.

'That's good,' he smiled, clearly taking her lack of a further response as confirmation of her willingness to collaborate with his scheme, 'all settled then,' and he reached out and stroked the backs of her smooth thighs while she stood dutifully before him, the shimmering front of her silk panties level with his face.

'Arthur...' she said carefully.

'Hm, what is it?' he responded, as though his mind was elsewhere, his eyes focussed on the tiny white triangle of silk just before them.

'I've been thinking about Christine,' she disclosed.

'You have?' he murmured. 'What about her?'

'You said she'd been trying to cause trouble to keep me away from Jack.'

'It seems that way, yes,' he confirmed. 'You want to be very careful where that girl's concerned.'

'Do you really think so?' she pressed, and he nodded inscrutably.

'Yes, I think so, and I'm not often wrong about people. Why?'

'I can't stop thinking about her,' she confessed. 'She was supposed to be my best friend.'

'I know, I know,' he said, 'but don't you worry yourself about treacherous people just now.'

Emily frowned, trying to dismiss her friend from her thoughts, his slowly rising hands distracting her.

'You really are a beautiful girl,' he said admiringly, eyeing the way the soft silk of her panties stretched over the gentle mound of her sex changed to various shades of white as he cupped and squeezed her buttocks, causing her to wince and inhale sharply as he traced her welts. Despite the sharp discomfort Emily felt her insides quake pleasurably as his fingers pressed into the warm curve of her panties. As he grasped her thighs again, just below the lower crease of her buttocks, and eased them apart, gently and slowly, she sensed he now wanted to masturbate her. Virtually naked in front of him, in his house, she again wasn't sure this could be right, but her nipples were stiffening and her clitoris was stirring within her moistening sex again. This was wrong, she sensed, but she'd vowed to obey him, she reflected. She'd promised to do exactly what he told her to do, and to keep him on her side she couldn't possibly go back on that again.

'Lie back on the sofa and relax,' he said, standing up and helping her recline as he directed. Then bending over her shapely form his hand glided across the smooth plain of her stomach, and without any further stalling slipped down beneath the elastic of her panties, and she murmured a faint denial as his fingers moved over and cupped the soft curls covering her sex. Emily gazed up at him, her eyes misty with tears of confusion, a myriad thoughts and doubts careering around the wreckage of her tormented mind as her insides quivered with shameful excitement. His hand was actually touching her sex, this time without even the flimsy barrier of her underwear to protect her shame. Where would this end? This couldn't be right - could it? Arthur was old enough to be her father. He was a longstanding friend of the family. Her parents trusted him, and she had trusted him. Surely this was wrong... wasn't it?

His fingers moved, daring to press between the lips of her pussy, and he caressed the sensitive tip of her erect clitoris. Emily trembled and tried to sit upright as he teased her. 'Just relax,' he whispered, a hand on her shoulder easing her down onto the sofa again as he cleverly massaged the sensitised core of her pleasure. 'Just relax and let yourself go.'

Closing her eyes, Emily knew this was what Arthur wanted. But did it matter?

She knew him well, and she was safe with him. She needed this release, and Arthur was only helping her achieve it. Parting her thighs a little more as her love lips were peeled further apart, her body trembled uncontrollably and she was aware of her juices anointing his working fingers. She knew she was already nearing her climax.

'You're doing well,' Arthur encouraged as he quickened his massaging rhythm. With her back arching and her breasts rising and falling, her breathing erratic, Emily dug her fingernails into the cushions as she teetered on the brink of her orgasm. With her head lolling from side to side she began whimpering in the grip of her pleasure. She was going to do it, she knew as her juices of arousal soaked his hand and the tight crotch of her panties. She was going to come.

'Yesss...' she breathed as her orgasm exploded within the bud of her clitoris. 'Oh, yesss...'

'That's it, keep coming,' Arthur coaxed, massaging her pulsating clitoris faster and faster. 'Keep coming, dear girl.'

'Oh yes,' she wailed. 'Please, don't stop.'

'I won't stop,' he assured her, gazing down victoriously at the shuddering beauty sprawled beneath him. 'Just keep coming for me.'

Lost in her sexual bliss, drifting through clouds of pure ecstasy, Emily shook violently as her orgasm peaked. Again and again shockwaves rocked her young body to the core as Arthur gradually slowed the friction of his fingers between her sex lips. Her tight panties held his hand snugly between her wet thighs, her clitoris alive beneath his thumb. Emily had never known such pleasure. The feel of a man's fingers masturbating her like that; never had she imagined the immense delight derivable from such attention.

Spinning questions of whether Arthur would make her masturbate him too drifted around her head. Did she want him to demand she do such a thing for him? No, it wouldn't be right.

With his free hand Arthur brushed her auburn hair away from her perspiring brow. He was gentle, knowing, understanding, as he ran his fingers down her cheek, traced the contours of her slender throat, and then down to circle her erect nipple.

'You're very wet,' he whispered, smiling as Emily opened her eyes. 'Did you enjoy that?'

'Yes,' she sighed as he pulled his hand from her panties and leaned down to place an affection kiss on her hot forehead.

'You'll feel better now I've released all that pent up tension,' he assured her. 'You'll feel relaxed and calm now.'

'I do,' Emily confirmed as her breathing slowed and her body began to calm. 'I do.' She should never have allowed her neighbour to do such a thing for her, but it was too late, she thought regretfully now her pleasure had subsided, the deed was done. No matter what happened now, no matter what the future held, never would she be able to erase the memory of Arthur masturbating her. Neither could she ever erase the fact that he had masturbated her, and never would he forget it.

Closing her eyes as she felt the front of her panties slipping down, she knew he was staring at the lips of her naked pussy. He was scrutinising her there, examining the most private part of her body. She could feel his fingers peeling her open, his gaze burning into the soft petals of her inner lips. Further he opened her, peering into the virginal entrance of her vagina. What did he intend to do now? Surely he wouldn't go any further, would he? Surely it was all over. Surely he'd achieved what he wanted. They couldn't go any further together. It wouldn't be right.

'You've taken another valuable step forward,' he said, his fingertips flitting around the pink lips of her sex.

'I'd better get dressed now,' she said. 'I'd better get home.'

'No,' he comforted, 'stay a while longer and relax. You can stay here a little longer.'

She wondered if his penis was erect, daring to glance quickly at his trousers, a dangerous frisson of secret excitement clutching her tummy as she saw they were still distorted at the front. Would he masturbate once she'd left his house? She thought he probably would.

Trying to clear her mind of such sinful images, Emily pondered her parents. They'd asked Arthur to keep an eye on her. They'd asked their trusted friend and neighbour to look after their daughter. Did that include seducing her? No, she rather doubted it did. But he had. He'd betrayed their trust, and she should hate him for it.

'I think I'd better be going now,' she said, the sensations induced by the fingers massaging her vagina and her breasts dangerously nice. She felt ashamed for finding pleasure in her neighbour's illicit groping.

'Soon,' he agreed, smoothing her panties back into place and concealing her shame. 'I'm just going to the bathroom. You relax there and then I'll see you home.'

'Oh, there's no need for you to do that—'

'Shhhh...' he soothed, 'I'll only be a few minutes.'

Feeling weary, snuggling into the comfy sofa, guilt consumed Emily as her head flooded with thoughts of what her next-door neighbour had just done to her. It was terribly wrong, but it was very nice. She shouldn't have allowed him to do it to her, but did it really matter? She'd enjoyed the experience, but now they'd gone this far he'd probably want to masturbate her again in the future and she didn't think that was a good idea. It wouldn't end there, she was sure.

Chapter 14

Emily was aware of movement in the room and slowly opened her eyes. 'No,' she shrieked, sitting up quickly and staring at Arthur standing naked before her, his penis spearing erect from his hairy groin. 'Arthur, what on earth do you think you're doing?'

'It's all right,' he said, pacifying her. 'It's perfectly all right.'

'No,' she disagreed, 'it isn't all right. It isn't all right at all. I think this has gone on far enough.'

'Emily, please don't start getting difficult now,' he warned.

'I'm not getting difficult,' she said, trying not to look at her neighbour's bobbing erection. 'But I am shocked.'

'I didn't want to have to push you, but seeing as there's very little time I don't have a choice,' he told her. 'I know we can continue even after your parents return, but we are going to have to get things moving. Do you understand that?'

'I'm not sure if I do, no,' she said.

'You have to trust me,' he urged. 'We've gone too far to turn back. Now, I want you to sit forward a little, towards the front edge of the sofa.'

'Arthur,' she said warily, 'this is not what I was expecting. I really don't think you should be standing naked in front of me like this.'

'I'm going to have to do some major covering up to keep you out of trouble,' he stated, his legs planted determinedly apart, his penis pulsing at her. 'You know that, don't you?'

'Yes, I do,' she said meekly, 'but—'

'Now I want you to touch my penis,' he instructed. 'Convince me I'll not be wasting my efforts. I want to help you, Emily, as I said I would, but I'm still not convinced about you. I need to be convinced.'

Staring at his throbbing organ, Emily's hands trembled on her thighs. Arthur looked down at her as she scrutinised his genitalia, the veined shaft bobbing gently in front of her spellbound face.

It was a shocking moment, but she had to stop deliberating, she knew. This was a pivotal moment in her life, and she had previously promised Arthur she'd do exactly as he told her.

'This is what it's all about,' Arthur said, moving closer to her. 'I thought you were ready for this before. But you shied away, didn't you?'

'I suppose I wasn't sure...' she responded, her eyes transfixed by his erection.

'You weren't sure?' he pressed.

'Oh, I don't know.'

'Come on, Emily, talk to me, be honest with me. Tell me what's on your mind.'

'I still have this nagging doubt,' she confessed shyly.

'That's what we're trying to deal with. Your embarrassment has gone, don't you agree?'

She considered this for a few moments. 'Yes, I suppose it has.'

'And the next thing to go will be your doubts,' he assured her. 'In a very short space of time you've already grown used to your nakedness in front of me. And once you've grown used to seeing me naked too, you'll be well on the way. Look how far you've come in a few days. When your parents went away you'd never had a man touch you, and you'd never seen a man naked. Just look how far you've come, Emily.'

'Yes, I know how far I've come,' she conceded. 'It's just that...'

'We started off on the wrong foot, and that was my fault. I had to spank you and ground you because I could see that, the way you were going, you'd land yourself in terrible trouble with your father. And if you're to stay out of trouble, I'm going to have to cover for you. Come on,' he urged, 'your doubts will soon go, my dear. Just touch me and see if they don't.'

'I suppose so,' she breathed.

'Feel my penis. I'm going to have to tell your father dreadful lies, Emily. You're reliant upon me to help you.'

'Yes... yes I realise that,' she stammered uncertainly.

'I don't like lying, Emily. It's not in my nature, but you can depend on me to cover for you.'

'I do appreciate that, Arthur,' she said. 'I know you're doing all this for my benefit.'

'That's good,' he said huskily. 'Then touch my penis, Emily. Touch it.'

Tentatively lifting one hand and reaching out, Emily gingerly ran her fingertips up and down the veined shaft and gasped as it lurched a little, growing, gradually rising even more to point directly at her flushed face. She owed Arthur a lot; he'd done so much to help her, and he was prepared to do more to help her. But now she was sitting virtually naked in his lounge feeling his penis, and that meant she needed him on her side more than ever. She was totally beholden now, because by doing this to him she was more in his power than ever before.

With his cock pulsing rhythmically against her tentative touch, his balls hanging within their sac between his thighs, she watched the purple globe and the little drop of liquid glistening from the small eye at the tip, and Arthur stifled a gasp of delight as her forefinger inquisitively ran over the silky-smooth surface of his swollen glans.

Instinctively grasping his shaft, feeling the warmth and hardness of it in her fist, she knew she was taking another step into the unknown. She wanted to turn back, but neither Arthur nor her instincts would let her. She had no intention of masturbating him, that was for sure; there was no way she was going to do that. But to keep him as her friend she would just do this for him, just stroke him a little more.

Watching his heavy scrotum swinging a little as she moved her hand up and down the veined stalk, she was fascinated by watching the foreskin rolling back and forth over his purple globe. Were all men so big? Her dainty fingers could barely meet around his girth.

'That's good,' Arthur breathed shakily. 'Now do it a little faster, my dear. Go on, do it a little faster.'

'I don't think I should...' she faltered, looking up at the pleasure etched in his expression. 'Arthur, I really don't think we should be doing this.'

'It's too late for silly doubts,' he grunted. 'You'll do as I say. It's all for your own good.'

Obediently moving her hand faster, Emily knew she shouldn't lift her other hand to cup and gently massage his balls, but she did. She knew he was going to ejaculate if she carried on and she didn't want that to happen, but she didn't stop, she did carry on. He began to breathe heavily, his naked body trembling as his knees sagged. She was actually masturbating her next-door neighbour. This was wrong; it had to be wrong. No matter what he said, no matter how he condoned or justified it, this was wrong. But there again, no one would ever know, she consoled herself. No one would ever know the price she'd paid to get and keep Arthur on her side.

What would her father say if he knew what she was doing? How would her mother react if she found out her innocent daughter had wanked their friend from next door, a man the same age as them?

'Don't stop,' Arthur gasped, his jaw clenching as he looked down at Emily's dainty fist moving up and down his cock.

'I don't think we should be doing this,' Emily repeated with little conviction, torn between right and wrong.

'That's good,' Arthur grunted, ignoring her words as his hips stabbed towards her face. 'That's very good. You're a natural, dear girl. Whatever you do don't *stop!*'

Her eyes wide with wonderment, Emily watched the creamy liquid erupt from the swollen tip of his cock, the first few eruptions arching into the air and spattering audibly against her cheek and her chin, making her flinch and blink with shock, the next few oozing down his straining cock and over her fingers as she continued to masturbate him. Arthur grunted and stabbed with his hips again, sending another eruption splattering onto the upper slopes of her naked breasts, where it seeped down into her cleavage and clung to her nipples. Arthur shuddered and moaned, his eruptions lessening in intensity, but still the mesmerised, inexperienced girl milked the last few drops from him.

With the flow of semen finally stemming Emily instinctively slowed her rhythm, moving her hand gently up and down the glistening shaft of her neighbour's penis as he loomed above her gasping with illicit pleasure. She'd done it, she realised. Right or wrong, she'd masturbated him to a climax, and although riddled with guilt, her thoughts confused, she felt secretly pleased with her efforts.

'That was very good,' Arthur praised her, his voice little more than a croak, his penis wilting before her sparkling eyes. 'I'm proud of you, Emily. I'm extremely proud of you.'

'Thanks,' she murmured, gazing at her fingers, coated with sperm.

'You know where the bathroom is if you want to clean up.'

Standing somewhat unsteadily and leaving the lounge, the sexual tension of what they'd done weakening her legs, Emily looked down at her sperm-encrusted breasts and inquisitively raised a fingertip to the drying discharge on her face as she climbed the stairs. This wasn't how she'd envisaged her first experience with a naked man, she thought, feeling numb. But again consoling herself with the thought that no one would ever know of their debauched activities together, she washed away the evidence of her neighbour's ejaculation - although she could never wash away the memory.

To her shock Arthur's penis was still semi-erect when she returned downstairs to the lounge. He was reclining nonchalantly in his armchair sipping from a glass of wine, still naked, his penis lying long and thick on his thigh. She'd hoped he'd be dressed by now, himself regretful of what they'd done and saying no more about it. But judging by his expression of arrogant contentment, he harboured no such regrets.

'I think I'd better be going now,' she said, trying to look anywhere but at him.

'Not yet, Emily,' he said, smiling at her as she hovered awkwardly by the door. 'There's no rush, is their? Tell me, how do you feel?'

'Well, I... I don't know,' she replied.

'You've come a long way, Emily. It's strange to think that we've known each other for all these years, and yet in just a few days we've got to know each other better than ever before; got closer than ever before. Yes, you've come a long way.'

'I have,' she agreed distractedly, wondering what this was leading to.

'Are you all right?' Arthur asked, suddenly frowning, his penis stirring a fraction on his thigh.

'To be honest,' Emily began, praying for him to stay in the armchair, 'I don't think you should be sitting there like that.'

'Like what?' he said. 'Naked, you mean?'

Emily nodded, suddenly finding herself wanting to talk, drawn into the room where she sat on the edge of the sofa, gazing uncomfortably down at the carpet.

'I told you, Emily,' he said firmly, 'you have to trust me. I know what's in your best interests.'

'It has nothing to do with trusting you,' she said, blushing as she raised her eyes and looked at the man, trying not to notice the way his penis spasmed a little towards his belly as he reclined there. 'I just think you should put your clothes on and I should go home.'

Arthur watched the hesitant girl for long, tense minutes, sipping his wine pensively, the heavy silence between them making her feel even more befuddled than ever. Then seeming to decide the moment was perfect for whatever he intended, he placed his glass on the occasional table beside his chair and stood up, his penis tilting upward a few degrees, swaying at the horizontal from his dark groin. He moved slowly, as though not wanting to startle a timid animal, and stood before her, his legs rooted slightly apart.

'You can go if you want to,' he quietly offered, but Emily just looked up into his face, uncertain, and remained sitting where she was.

'Okay, if you're not going I want you to kneel on the floor,' he ordered, and even he looked a little surprised as, almost trancelike, she followed his command and slipped to her knees in the narrow space between his feet and the front of the sofa. With his penis stiffening even more mere inches from her clear, mesmerised face, she gazed again upon the foreboding organ. The veined shaft throbbed and the purple crown swelled, and it pointed with intent at her slightly

117

parted lips.

'Open your mouth,' he instructed her, but she shook her head, her eyes still glued to the threatening column of flesh before them.

'Arthur, I...' she whispered, her sweet breath wafting over his bloated tip, making him shudder with the promise of what was to come.

'I intend to teach you how to perform oral sex, Emily,' he told her frankly.

'No, this is wrong,' she whispered, a tear rolling down her flushed cheek as her wide eyes gazed beseechingly up at him.

'Wrong?' he echoed, focusing on her succulent lips and moving in closer to her. 'But this is what you want,' he told her. 'If we're talking about right or wrong, it would be wrong of me not to give you the benefit of my experience. You're a beautiful girl, Emily, which makes you vulnerable. You're naïve and inexperienced. There's no telling what trouble you might get into if I were to neglect my responsibilities now. I'm here to help you, my dear,' he said again, smiling down at her. 'I'm here to look after you, to keep you out of trouble. Now just open your mouth a little. We'll take it slowly. If you're unsure about it we'll stop.'

Staring at his bulbous knob as he inched his hips forward, the silky surface of his glans mere inches from her pouting, slightly open mouth, Emily felt her heart thumping in her chest, her stomach churning, her hands trembling.

'Here, I'll help you,' he whispered, and pressing a hand to the back of her head, his fingers entwining in her silky hair to gain purchase, and using the thumb of his other hand to press down on her chin and open her mouth a little further, he leaned in and fed the swollen plum of his cock just a little between her soft lips. He paused, allowing the girl to grow accustomed to the feel of him in her mouth. Instinctively opening wider, allowing his glans to enter her, she tasted his salty pre-come and breathed in the masculine scent of his groin. His bulbous tip seemed huge, filling her mouth, pressing out against one cheek. This couldn't be right, she again thought as his penis swelled, his pubic hair agitating her nose as he sank his erection even deeper into her warm mouth, her lips stretched tautly around his solid shaft as his tip nudged the back of her throat, and she knew there was no turning back now.

'Use your tongue,' he instructed, his voice taut, his thigh muscles tensed. 'You must learn, Emily, how to please a man with your mouth.' Slowly releasing her chin and moving his hand to the back of her head with his other, he began to gently rock his hips, repeatedly sinking his swollen helmet to the back of her throat as she breathed valiantly through her nose. 'Lick it,' he grunted. 'Lick it and suck it. That's nice... that's very nice...'

With her mind spinning Emily closed her eyes. He wouldn't come in her mouth, would he? He was teaching her, giving her the benefit of his experience, but surely he wouldn't go *that* far? Lost in her confusion, Emily shamefully heard the wet sounds as she obediently sucked and licked her neighbour's erect penis. His breathing was fast and shallow, his rigid penis throbbing and stretching her lips wider, and with him looming over her, pressing her face tight against his groin as she knelt between his parted legs, she felt humble and submissive.

Suddenly he began to tremble uncontrollably, gasping as the velveteen surface of his glans repeated nudged the back of her throat. Sucking diligently and dutifully she wondered what sperm would taste like. Should she swallow it?

'Suck,' Arthur demanded urgently, quickening his thrusting rhythm, then clamping his fingers into her scalp and jerking his groin against her flushed face he looked up at the ceiling with bulging eyes and let out a long, low moan of pleasure. 'Swallow it,' he ordered the girl, 'swallow it all,' and then salty sperm jetted from his spasming penis and filled her mouth, a little overflowing from the corner of her stretched lips, the substance dribbling down her chin... and Emily swallowed.

Again the penis filling her mouth spat into her throat, and the kneeling girl drank from her neighbour, his twitching balls rolling against her chin as he penetrated her to the root, his talon-like fingers holding her head still.

The panting man swayed on his sagging legs as the girl swallowed the last of his sperm. With his penis finally wilting he staggered back, his spent cock flopping from between her sperm-coated lips, and slumped back into the armchair, leaving her kneeling alone, bemused, her head bowed.

'That was very good,' he finally wheezed as she wearily lifted herself back up onto the sofa. 'You did very well, my dear. You're a very quick learner.'

'I think I'd better go now,' she said again, the distinctive taste of sperm lingering on her tongue.

'No, no, don't go yet,' he said.

'But I must,' she insisted.

'No, stay for a while longer.'

Sighing, Emily lifted her eyes and gazed at his dormant penis as he smiled lazily across at her. What had she done? Sucking her neighbour's penis was shameful. And yet, she had to admit the experience had sent her senses soaring.

Arthur pensively sipped his wine in silence, scrutinising her closely through narrowed eyes as she sat looking down at her hands, clasped lightly together in her lap. Then, when his glass was empty he placed it again on the small table beside his chair and crept across to the silent girl. He knelt in front of her knees, and she looked at him with an expression of inquisitive acceptance on her lovely face.

Emily was about to lose her virginity, she knew, and she was strangely resigned to that knowledge. To be anything else would be pointless. As Arthur lifted his hands to her knees and pressed, prising her thighs gently apart, she even reclined on the sofa without being told to, watching him cautiously. Did she want to lose her virginity? She didn't think she did, but she knew she was going to. Did she want to lose her virginity to her older neighbour? Again she didn't think she did, but again, she knew she was going to.

'No,' she gasped as he leaned between her spread thighs and pressed his mouth to the lips of her sex through her silk panties. She hadn't expected that, but ignoring her feeble protest he pressed the tip of his tongue into her entrance and licked her there, through the silk. Emily shuddered, her mind blown away with conflicting confusion and arousal as he used a finger and thumb to peel the damp material aside and ran his tongue deftly around the awakening nub of her sensitive clitoris. Although the sensations were amazing, Emily found it almost impossible to accept that her neighbour was actually kneeling between her legs, his face buried between her thighs, his tongue licking her sex, but she squealed with illicit pleasure, her back arched and she instinctively buried her fingers into his greying hair as he suddenly drove his tongue into the wet heat of her vagina.

'No,' she again murmured, unsure of her real feelings as he licked and probed her defenceless pussy. She shouldn't be doing this; she shouldn't be gleaning sexual pleasure from her neighbour's tongue.

'Relax and enjoy it,' Arthur breathed, pulling his mouth back slightly from her glistening sex lips. 'Relax and enjoy feeding off my experience, Emily.'

'Arthur, please...' she pleaded as she felt another shameful orgasm simmering in the pit of her tummy.

'Trust me,' he told her again, giving her sensitive sex petals a possessive kiss. 'Trust me, my dear. Everything will be fine...'

Emily had lost the meaning of trust. She *had* trusted Arthur completely, and because of that trust she was now naked in his lounge with him kneeling between her legs and his tongue licking her clitoris. Shockingly close to her unforgivable orgasm she dug her fingertips into his head, the slurping sounds of oral sex filling her ears and mortifying her. Rolling her head back and closing her eyes, she knew she was going to come. Gasping, her nubile body writhing on his sofa, she knew she was going to cross the threshold and shudder in an inexcusable, tongue-induced orgasm. Through swirling emotions she knew she could halt this illicit act - if she wanted to; she could push the man away and flee his house. But the unfamiliar sensations were driving her wild.

'*No!*' she squealed, her clitoris exploding in bliss within Arthur's hungry mouth. Her body shaking violently, incredible sensations rocking her very soul, her knuckles turned white as she clung to his head and rode the crest of her climax.

Images of her parents loomed in the turmoil of her mind as she gasped and whimpered in her forbidden release. Her father wagging his finger, scolding her, her mother with her hands on her hips, a look of sheer disgust depicted in her angry expression. Her orgasm peaking, her sex juices anointing the man's mouth and chin, she cried out in the grip of her unforgivable lust.

'No more,' she gasped. 'God, no... I can't take any more...' Another wave of intense sexual pleasure washed through her shuddering, exhausted form, and she thought she was going to pass out from the pleasure. She was slumped against the back of the sofa, her breasts rising and falling raggedly as she breathed deeply, her smooth flesh bathed in a sheen of perspiration.

'No...' the exhausted girl whispered as Arthur shuffled closer on his knees and pulled her limp calves back around his thighs. Through half open eyes she watched him place his hands on her thighs and press them further apart. Then he squeezed his hands between her buttocks and the sofa, and with ease he pulled her closer to him so that her knees were wedged apart by his hips, closer to where his penis again stood erect, spearing up over the gentle mound of her soft, naked pubic nest.

'Now, my dear,' he said hoarsely, kneeling tall over her shattered, supine form, his hands smoothing up to grip the tops of her thighs, holding her just where he wanted her, pinned at his mercy on the sofa, 'at last we reach the conclusion of this stage of your education.'

'Arthur, please...' she whispered futilely, watching as he dipped his hips a little and the smooth, purple glans slipped just between the engorged petals of her sex lips, pressing through the wet, white silk of her panties. Then he paused, gazing down at the beautiful girl spread before him.

'Are you ready, young lady?' he asked. 'I'm going to fuck you now. You may not be aware, but I've been waiting for this moment for quite some time. And you're going to enjoy it too. Your parents going on holiday couldn't have fallen in line with my plans more perfectly. From the moment your father told me of their holiday I've been waiting for this moment, preparing for it.' As he spoke his hips moved forward a little and the bulbous globe of his erection nosed a little further between her sex lips, the delicate silk the only barrier between him and her virginity, and the trapped girl, gazing up at the man through misty eyes, gasped and stiffened, waiting tensely for the inevitable, her hands anxiously clamped to the sofa cushions.

'I love the feel of your silk panties against my cock,' he whispered. 'I'm pleased I bought them for you; we'll have some more fun with them later,' he promised, and moved his thumbs to ease the silk to one side, open her sex lips wider and push his cock-head an inch or so inside her tight, virginal channel, 'but I need to fuck you now.'

Emily held her breath and watched him, not daring to move, not able to move.

'Are you ready?' he said, Emily noticing the veins standing out on his temples as he held himself ready to penetrate her.

'I think so,' she whispered bravely. 'If you really have to do this...'

'I do, my dear,' he told her. 'Believe me, I do. I've waited long enough, and now it's my moment.'

The man and the girl stared into each other's eyes for tense seconds, and then he stabbed with his hips and she stiffened on the sofa as he impaled her with one, long, steady thrust. She instinctively lifted her knees to squeeze his flanks and her hands to press against his hairy chest in one last silent rebellion, only her bottom and her shoulders touching the sofa as her back arched, the lithe movement lifting her firm breasts for him to drool over and inadvertently allowing his cock a better angle into her superb, tight young body. His groin pressed tightly against hers, their pubic hair mingling, and the pinned girl opened her mouth in a silent exclamation against the alien violation.

'It's all right,' he gasped, his swollen glans pressing deep inside her body. 'It's all right, dear girl. Relax... just relax and enjoy it.'

121

This was it, Emily thought in her torment. He was taking her virginity. This was where the path led. Arthur had coaxed her along that path, toyed with her, manipulated her, and now the solid shaft of his penis was embedded deep within the hugging sheath of her vagina.

With his juice-glistening shaft slowly withdrawing, Emily looked down aghast at the forbidden coupling. Her sex lips were stretched tautly around the veined organ, the plum of his helmet lodged just inside her, and then she gasped and watched in awe as his rigid penis slowly disappeared, sinking into her again, gliding deep, opening her tight channel, inch after glistening inch of the solid stem vanishing into the hot depths of her vanquished body.

The man then started fucking the girl, rocking in and out of her as she moaned and writhed beneath him on his sofa. He grunted, his brow beaded with sweat, his eyes bulging as he quickened his thrusting motions, his movements becoming increasingly ragged. He was fucking her with dire determination, and as Emily stared up into his grimacing face she knew he was close to coming, that he fully intended to come inside her.

'Arthur,' she gasped, her firm breasts quivering as he shunted her body back and forth on the sofa. 'Arthur, you mustn't. You can't... you can't come inside me.' But the man was beyond listening and earnestly squeezed her waist in both hands, pulling her more desperately onto his stiff pole, and despite her fears Emily felt her clitoris responding deliciously. Stimulated beyond belief by the powerful male shaft thrusting in and out of her, she knew she was about to orgasm again too. She teetered on the verge of her climax, impaled upon her next-door neighbour's bludgeoning erection, the last shreds of innocence finally stripped from her.

'I'm coming,' Arthur croaked through gritted teeth, his thrusting cock swelling even more, stretching Emily's tight vagina. Then, with her own climax exploding from the bulb of her clitoris, she was just aware of his seed erupting deep inside her. She rolled her head from side to side and pressed her knuckles against her open mouth to suppress the scream of joy threatening to wrench from her lungs. She was no longer a virgin, her veil of innocence stripped away by the wind of lust like autumn leaves, tears seeping from her closed eyes and meandered down her cheeks, where they dripped and soaked into her neighbour's sofa.

'You've done it, you beautiful thing,' Arthur breathed heavily, his shoulders slumped with fatigue, his penis still stiff and buried in the clutching depths of her vagina. 'You've really done it...'

Through swirling thoughts Emily pondered his words as her orgasm ebbed. The day of her deflowering had come, but never had she thought it would be like this.

'And you were very, very good,' he drooled shakily as she gazed down beyond her perspiring breasts and watched his wilting penis withdraw from her wet vagina. 'Did you enjoy it?'

'I... I don't know,' she replied softly, as his purple globe flopped out from between her tender sex lips and made her gasp a little. 'Maybe... I'm not sure.'

'Oh, I think you did,' he chuckled arrogantly. 'I think you did.'

'But you shouldn't have come inside me like that,' she protested wearily. 'You shouldn't have done that. You should have pulled out.'

'I don't think so,' he said. 'I'd defy any red-blooded male to pull out of a gorgeous girl like you at the crucial moment.' He shook his head and idly stroked her thigh with one hand and her flushed cheek with the palm of the other as she pulled herself up into more of a sitting position. 'No, my dear, that wasn't an option at all, I'm afraid.'

'I want to go home now, please,' she said jadedly.

'Nonsense,' he said. 'After what we've just experienced together? No, you're going to stay here with me tonight.'

Emily shook her head, wanting to put her clothes on and get back to the sanctuary of her own home. 'No Arthur, I really want to go—'

'Shhhh...' he hushed her, placing his forefinger over her soft lips. 'You're staying with me tonight, and that's an end to it. You'll stay with me in my room... in my bed.'

Emily slowly shook her head in disbelief of what she was hearing, silenced by the presence of his finger, but even when he removed it and stood up, took her hand and guided her to her feet, she still said nothing more.

He led her out into the hall to the foot of the unlit stairs. Then he murmured quiet words of comfort and encouragement and started to lead her upwards by the hand, and despite gazing apprehensively up into the darkness beyond his open bedroom door, she began to see things more clearly in her mind.

Upstairs, as Emily stood gazing down at the squat shadow of his double bed, waiting for her like some foreboding sacrificial altar, she began to understand.

As she lay on her side beneath the quilt, her knees drawn up protectively, gazing at but not seeing the orange glow from the streetlight outside trying to creep around the closed curtains, she knew there never had been any report book.

As she heard the bedroom door close, a wooden barrier between them and the outside world, she knew the phone didn't have a fault on the line; she knew Arthur had sabotaged it.

As she felt the mattress sag and Arthur's body squeeze close against her back, his thighs tucked up beneath hers, an arm slipping over her waist, a hand creeping up her tummy to maul her breasts, his lips nuzzling her neck and ear, his dormant penis sandwiched against her silk panties, she knew why her father hadn't mentioned to her that he'd lost eighty pounds from his wallet; because he *hadn't* lost eighty pounds from his wallet.

As hands moved to the waist of her panties and smoothed them down her legs she knew her father had never discovered her masturbating; that her neighbour had successfully gambled on a bluff.

As he whispered in her ear, telling her exactly what he was going to do to her, his erection seemingly stimulated by his lewd commentary and pulsing between her buttocks, she knew her parents had never given him the telephone number of their hotel in Spain. She knew there was nobody on the other end of the line when he stood in his hall and phoned, that she'd fallen for another bluff.

As hands turned her over to face him and urged her down into the darkness beneath the quilt, with gruff instructions to get him 'ready' and crude comments that she had a great mouth and should use it more, she knew that Chrissie, her best friend, was not chasing Jack and had not betrayed her.

As she lay curled in the humid darkness beneath his bedding, obediently kissing his belly, his thighs, feeling his flaccid penis unfurling against her cheek, she knew Chrissie had not telephoned her parents telling tales on her.

As he rolled lazily onto his back and threw aside the quilt so he could exult in watching her carry out his wishes, she knew he'd never called round to see Chrissie's mother to tell fabricated accusations about her and Chrissie's dad.

As he pulled her over his groin, his rejuvenated erection sprouting at an angle over his belly and pressing against her lips, demanding entry, stretching them wide and then possessively moving languidly in and out of her mouth, she knew her father had not been ringing him from Spain to check up on her.

As he halted her with another grunt, grumbling that she was taking him too far too quickly, cruelly remarking that she was a natural cock-sucker then rolling her over onto her back, she knew who had planted the vibrator in her bed and taken those incriminating photographs.

As he brusquely pushed her legs apart and heaved himself between them, his erection buffeting her trembling tummy, his chest pressing against her breasts, the greying hair rasping against her traitorously erect nipples, she knew.

As he fumbled and groped, panted against her shoulder and managed to position his erection just between her sex lips, she knew.

As Emily gazed up at the shadowy ceiling above; as she bore the weight of her next-door neighbour, sandwiched between him and the sagging mattress; as she heard him mutter in her ear that he was going to fuck her again, that she was his now; as she lifted her hands and clutched the pillows in readiness; as he stabbed with his hips and fulfilled his hoarse pledge to fuck her again with his long, stiff cock, she understood everything with absolute clarity.

www.ingramcontent.com/pod-product-compliance
Lightning Source LLC
Chambersburg PA
CBHW060939120626
46557CB00003B/1065